IN TOO DEEP

BAILEY B

ISBN: 978-1-959724-13-1

Discrete Cover ISBN: 978-1-959724-14-8

Ebook: 978-1-959724-10-0

ASIN: B0BL5WYWFG

❀ Created with Vellum

For every girl who's fallen in love with their best friend

Chapter 1

HARPER

I PULL a cigarette from a newly purchased pack of Marlboro Reds and light it up. I close my eyes on an inhale, letting the smoke singe my lungs, and then open them on the exhale. It's been over a year since I've smoked anything, let alone had a drink. The sensation of having the filter between my lips is unnerving and claiming at the same time.

It's a distraction, which is what I need.

There's music playing on the hotel's pool deck. Tiny hidden speakers sing loud enough that each song can be heard at every beach chair, but not so loud people can't talk. From where I sit at the bar, the guests in the reserved party area are doing just that.

Talking.

Drinking.

Having the time of their lives.

I should be over there, relishing in the pre-wedding festivities, but I can't bring myself to leave my stool. For thirty minutes I've sat here, watching the people I used to call friends mingle. Each face is the same, with minor differences.

Laugh lines around the lips. Tired eyes. A few new tattoos. All in all, they haven't changed.

I have.

"Fancy seeing you here."

Noah Ruckers. Best friend, but not. A man I gave all my firsts to, and thoroughly let down over the years. For a moment, everything inside me tenses. Eighteen months have passed since I last saw his face. Five hundred and forty-eight days where I almost caved when things got hard. Seven hundred and seventy-nine thousand minutes (give or take).

I've lost count of how many times I almost asked him if I could come home. Or thought about begging him to come visit me.

I didn't do either.

Not for my sake, but his.

Noah takes a seat at the open barstool beside me. He reaches for my hair, a deep shade of brown with royal blue ends, and his finger brushes across my bare shoulder.

"Your hair is different." He smiles and something warm pools in my stomach when he adds, "It looks nice."

I mumble, "Thanks," and reach for my water. It's cold but does nothing to ease the ache in my chest. I itch to hug him, but keep my distance. For one, I'm not one hundred percent sure where we stand. I've been a shit friend since I left, avoiding all meaningful communication and resorting to bi-weekly *you doing good* texts.

Mainly, though, my not-so-best-friend looks fucking fine and it's tripping me out.

Noah has always been attractive, but there's something different today. I can't put my finger on it, but I can't stop looking. Maybe it's the fact that most days his wardrobe consists of a T-shirt and jeans unless we were going to the beach, then it is board shorts and bare skin, and today he's dressed to the nines. The pressed button-down with the sleeves rolled up and dark blue slacks that hug his ass look good.

So good that my cigarette misses my mouth when I bring it to my lips. Noah chuckles at my clumsiness and I laugh too, embarrassed. I set the cig in the ashtray, temporarily giving up on using smoking to calm my nerves. My hair slips from between his fingers.

I chew on my bottom lip, unsure of what to do now. The divide between us is thick. It hangs in the air, draped in unspoken truths.

We stare at each other, with nothing to say because at this point, where do we even start?

Last Noah knew, I was living outside of Savannah and working at a dentist office. He has no idea I work at two all night diners and barely scrape by. Or that I used last month's rent to pay for this weekend's hotel and have been living out of my car ever since. So much about our lives has been left out of our texts, I'm not sure it can be said we even *know* each other any more.

I look down to the ashtray and frown. My cigarette has turned into a stick of ash. A metaphor for my life. One minute everything is fine, I'm cruising along, and the next my plans are derailed and I've been discarded.

I pull two new cigs from my pack and offer Noah one. I think he still smokes. I can't remember him saying anything about quitting. Then again, that could have been one of those not so little details left out of our conversations on his end.

He shakes his head. "I thought you quit?"

I light mine and take a deep inhale. The way his gaze skirts over my body makes me nervous. Not in a bad way, just... I don't know. I'm overthinking things today.

"I did, right after I left." I hold my breath until I can't take the burn in my chest anymore, then release the smoke. "But being back has got me more stressed out than a mother with newborn twins screaming their lungs out at Wal-Mart."

"Nice comparison." He chuckles, the sound deep in his throat, and I find myself looking down at the bar top to fight a smile.

I like the way it sounds.

It reminds me of the old days when Noah and I were still in high school, and shit was easy. When life consisted of late nights at the local diner, riding our bikes down the boardwalk, and stopping at a hotel bar to drink Shirley Temples and share a basket of fries.

Dark memories I've worked hard to lock away creep up on me. I can't help but wonder, *What would have happened if we didn't break up? Or what if we had gotten back together in college, like we'd planned, and I never dated Rob... where would my life be?*

I force the corners of my lips to stay upturned and bat my lashes. Flirting with Noah is an easy distraction. I don't think I could forget how to if I tried. It's harmless, shameless flirting, but it used to piss my ex-boyfriend off. Not that that matters anymore.

"What can I say?" I shrug and lean closer until our shoulders touch. "I'm a master of words."

"Hi, there. I'm Misha. Can I get you anything?" the bartender interrupts.

Misha leans one arm on the counter, giving Noah a perfect view of her tits. I roll my eyes as his gaze settles on her rack for the briefest of moments, then finds her face. He lifts his lips into a lazy smile, one that used to make my heart race.

Still makes my heart race, even if I wish it wouldn't.

"I'll have a glass of Jameson," Noah says, his country-boy accent thicker than molasses. I don't know where his twang comes from. He's a beach bum with salt water in his veins and his family is Florida bred, but there are times he sounds more southern than a cowboy in the thick of Alabama.

An unfamiliar squeezing sensation catches me off guard. It swells in my chest until each breath is a struggle. I let out the air in my lungs, counting to five before trying to inhale. After two cycles, I realize this feeling doesn't stem from my anxiety.

It's something else.

Something I vaguely recognize and almost laugh once I pinpoint what it is. I take another drag off my cig and try to ignore it. I like to flirt with Noah, I like to see his cheeks flush red. He, in return, pushes my buttons in the best of ways. It's who we are—well, were before I left. We both know our banter means nothing. It's harmless.

And yet, I'm jealous.

This is going to be a long ass weekend.

"Mmm," Misha hums, practically salivating. "Honey, with that accent you can have *anything* you want." She writes her number on a napkin square then slides it and the drink Noah ordered across the bar. The woman winks and then, thankfully, goes to throw herself, I mean wait, on her other guests.

Noah looks at the napkin square. He chuckles as he picks it up and then crumbles it into a ball. He spins on his stool and leans against the bar top. For a minute, he stares out at the crowd of people I'm avoiding.

My heart beats in anticipation. I can feel unspoken questions lingering between us. Am I okay? What's it going to be like to see Rob, my ex, again? There are a million variations of those two questions that have been asked to avoid saying the words everyone wants to ask.

Am I going to relapse by being here?

Noah downs his drink in two big swallows, then sets the glass on the counter behind him. "Are you ready to face the wolves?"

I turn in my seat and catch sight of our bartender again. Even across the bar, she's still watching Noah, shooting me the stink eye whenever our gazes meet. I laugh a little and choose to focus on that sensation, the pride of her not knowing what's going on between Noah and I—which is nothing—instead of worrying about what hasn't been said yet.

I glance across the pool deck again, my gaze searching and finding a set of tattoos before seeing the owner's face. His back is to me, but I'd know the enormous shamrock tattoo on the back of his arm anywhere, even with a sleeve of artwork surrounding it.

Robert Peterson.

The man who made me and broke me all at once.

It's been almost two years since we broke up. I spent five months in rehab and moved away to start over and rebuild myself so that if this day ever came I would be ready. I *should* be okay… and yet, my stomach cramps at the sight of my ex-boyfriend's tattoos.

Not even his face.

I close my eyes with my next inhale of my cigarette, unwanted memories slipping through the cracks of my tough-girl-facade. They say that time heals all wounds, but those people—whoever they are—have never had a cut run deep into their soul. They've never felt their heart bleed and bleed until there is nothing left. They don't understand what it's like to fall in love with the wrong man and completely lose yourself.

They have never been broken beyond repair.

I fight a wave of unexpected tears and choke on the smoke in my lungs like a kid puffing on my first cig. My hand goes to my chest to beat clean air into my body. Noah grabs my water and pats my back. He's ready, as always, to take care of me and the guilt is more than I can bear.

"We don't have to—"

"I'm fine." I cut him off and snatch my water from his hand. I finish it and set the cup behind me. "I've got this."

Noah looks skeptical but he stretches his arms and leans his elbows on the bar. The last few times I saw him, his dark hair was short and gelled up in the front, but it's different now, a little longer, curling around his freckled ears. "Whatever you say, princess."

"Don't call me that."

"Whatever you say, *Harper*." Noah takes my hand in his. Green eyes suck me in with a look of interest I never thought I'd see again. I don't like it…but I also don't hate it either.

Fuck. This is confusing.

I roll my eyes and tug free of his grasp. I grab the hair tie from my wrist and twist my locks into a messy bun because my fingers were semi-accidentally close to his nether regions and it's making me feel weird. Tingly. "Princesses need saving, and I'm not that girl anymore."

Noah's jaw drops. He gasps dramatically and covers his heart with his hand, like a lovesick cartoon character. "Damn. You mean I won't get to be your knight in shining armor during this shitshow of a wedding?"

"Shut up, you idiot."I bite back a grin and punch Noah in the shoulder, not expecting my fist to collide with solid muscle. I wince and shake my hand, which earns me yet another chuckle from him.

Noah looks me dead in the eye, demanding my attention. "For reals, though, Harper. You look amazing. Whatever you've done since you've been gone has worked. I wish you'd call more, but I'm proud of you. "

My cheeks flush. It's been a long time since anyone said they were proud of me, well anyone that counts. My therapist told me she was proud on discharge day, but she was paid to say that. So, I took her compliment with a grain of salt and I cut everyone else out of my life who's opinion might have mattered.

"Wow. Way to make things weird and sappy," I tease, failing at ignoring the tornados in my stomach. Noah cracks another smile, his eyes lighting up. *Fuck, he's beautiful.*

I can't hear the clank of a spoon against a glass, but I can see Ethan Johnson—the man of the night—gathering everyone at the party area in a circle.

It's time.

I snuff out what's left of my current cigarette and reach for another. Tiny tremors take control of my body and the little hairs on the back of my neck stand on edge. I thought I was prepared to see everyone again, but now that it's time… I'm not ready. I don't think I can stand beside the people I called friends and smile and act like nothing happened.

God. I'm so stupid. I shouldn't have come here tonight.

I should go back to Georgia before anyone else realizes I've made the trip.

I should…

"Hey." Noah sets his hand on top of mine and squeezes to catch my attention.

I look up at him, a heartbeat away from a full-blown panic attack. I open my mouth to tell him I'm fine, but the words catch in my throat. I think about the pills in my hotel room, and how I haven't needed them for months; but I want one. I want to chase away the anxiety of what this trip will do to me and drown it all with a martini. My therapist's words echo in my head, *take them with you. Just in case.*

"Deep breath, Harper. Like this." Noah sucks in a gulp of air, holds it, then releases slowly.

I know the technique but my thoughts are jumping from one thing to the next. Gemma will hate me if I leave. I told her I'd come. I promised.

I can't see Rob again.

I can't.

I...

"Harper!" Noah snaps. I find his gaze again and he says. "Breathe, woman. Just breathe."

I copy his motions, forcing my body to cooperate. After six cycles of slow, exaggerated breaths, my heart slows to a semi-normal pace and the paralyzing grip around my senses dissipates. I look down at my hands, embarrassed at my inability to control my emotions and that I can't make them stop shaking.

"Are you okay?" he asks.

I can't lie to Noah. He'll see right through me if I try. That man could always read my tells like I was a book. Knowing my luck, he still can. Honestly, after everything I've put him through, I'm surprised he's by my side acting as if the last few years never happened. I owe him the truth simply out of respect for how he's treating me now.

So I don't say anything.

Noah takes my silence for what it is and slides off the barstool. He holds his elbow out to me. I smile, grateful he isn't pushing for an answer I don't have as I tuck what's left of my pack of cigarettes into my boot.

"I'm not ready," I tell him honestly, linking my arm through his.

Noah squeezes my hand and meets my gaze. His eyes are tired, sad, and lacking the vibrancy I remember. I feel bad, wondering if I'm part of the cause. I can't begin to imagine what Noah's life is like these days, but for a while I know I was the cause of more than a few sleepless nights.

"You already did the hard part, Harper. You showed up. Everything else will be cake in comparison." Noah's lip lifts in the corner. It's not the same lazy smile that made my pulse race, but this one does something to me too.

Chapter 2

HARPER

MY HEART BEATS FASTER with each step. I can't tell if I'm going to pass out or throw up, but I don't feel good. I focus my gaze on the concrete, a few feet ahead of us, and count the cracks. It helps with the anticipation, like when you close your eyes as the roller coaster cart *tick tick ticks* its way to the top of the first drop.

Less than ten feet from the designated party area, Noah stops. He turns, putting himself between everyone and me, and blocks my view. His hands slide up my arms to cup my face, long fingers tangling into my roots.

Shock pushes its way through all the other emotions. I can't breathe, and not because I'm freaking out. Noah's touch literally sucks the air from my lungs while sending a jolt of electricity through my veins. He tilts my head and looks me in the eye. The crazy thought that he might kiss me crosses my mind and I realize, I want him to.

I stare at his lips and try to remember what they felt like all those years ago. I don't find the memories I'm looking for. Instead, I'm hit with a horde of emotions I never expected to feel.

Anxiousness.

Excitement.

And the weirdest of all... desire.

The deep rumble of Noah's voice breaks through the fog that smothers my sanity. This is crazy. I shouldn't be tempted to lean into him. I shouldn't want to skip today's meet and greet lunch and take him up to my room.

I *should* have hooked up with the guy from that bar in Atlanta last weekend. Apparently my three-week dry spell is messing with my head.

"Whatever you need, Harper, I'm here for you." Noah pointedly looks me in the eyes. He's so close. His breath smells of whiskey and mint. *God, I want to taste him.* "I mean it. Anything."

I feel like there's a message between the lines I'm missing, or maybe I just want there to be. I stare at him a second longer, then decide I'm looking too deep into nothing. Noah is just being, well, Noah, while I'm over here losing my mind.

I smile, not wanting to seem ungrateful for the offer even though I don't fully understand it. "Thank you."

Noah drops his arms and re-tangles his fingers with mine. I look down at our hands, remembering how we used to walk the halls like this. What I don't remember is a buzz of electricity flowing from my palm to my chest.

That buzz is here, stronger than anything I ever felt with Rob, and I loved that man with all my heart.

I let him guide us across the threshold of the pre-wedding weekend gathering. Everyone in the ceremony is supposed to meet this afternoon. Gemma's logic is that it would make the evening events less awkward. Not sure if I agree with her, but it's not my big weekend.

In fact, if this were my wedding, I would have done a lot of things differently, starting with the rehearsal. She's not having one, which to me is crazy. I need to know where she wants me to stand, who I'm walking with and what the plan is if it rains. This is Florida! Assuming it's not going to rain is as stupid as walking outside and not expecting to get a sun burn.

What boggles my mind even more is that Gemma has been dreaming about her wedding since before we met. I'm talking vision books, fabric swatches, the works. I was given no guidance on a bridesmaid dress; color, style, length, nada. No direction for how she wants my hair and makeup. As for shoes... we're going barefoot!

Who is this woman? And what happened to the girl I used to call my bestie while I was gone?

The Gemma I knew was a thinker. A planner. The kind of girl who couldn't stand a spec of dirt in her house and had everything in her pantry labeled. Her hair and makeup was always runway ready. Even after pushing out an eight-pound baby, she looked ready to take on the world, glistening with joy.

She is the *Nailed It* kind of woman, whereas I'm the failed attempt to recreate. The picture that turns into a meme because everything went horribly wrong.

But Gemma was also the type of person who put everyone before herself, almost to a fault. She wore her heart on her sleeve, never having an ill word to say about someone unless they deserved it and it was to their face. Most importantly, she never gave up on me.

That Gemma is why I've shoved my ghosts into a closet to brave this weekend.

Speaking of those ghosts, the horniest one of them all is headed my way, beer in hand. The nervous butterflies fluttering about my stomach mutate into angry cats—clawing at my insides. I knew Rob and I would have to interact this weekend, but I was hoping his conscience would keep him far away.

I should have known better.

"Damn, Harper. You look good." Rob's brown eyes trail over my body, down to my toes. His gaze stills on the v-neck plunge of my shirt, and then finds my face again. I hate the way he's looking at me. I've known him so long, I can practically hear what he's thinking and I want no part of it. "I hardly recognized you."

"Thanks."

"Hey, man," Noah says, putting himself in our conversation. "Long time."

"Yeah," Rob replies, but he has no interest in Noah. His gaze hasn't left my face. He's waiting for me to ask him a question, probably how he's doing. Or maybe ask what's new in his life. Something to break the ice, but the last thing I want is to make small talk.

I reach into my boot, simply to have something to do, besides awkwardly stare at my ex, and grab my pack of smokes before my ghosts can get the best of me. I stick a cigarette in my mouth and search for the matchbook that seems to have fallen under my foot.

Noah pulls out a lighter, probably from his own pack of smokes, and flicks his thumb against the wheel.

Once.

Twice.

And then there's fire. I lean forward, the end of my cigarette finding a dancing flame, and inhale. My throat tickles, burning with the need to expel the toxins from my body with a cough, but I relish the feeling. When the ember burns red, Noah's hand retracts. His lighter returns to wherever it came from and I stand up straight.

I blow out a cloud of smoke and flick my ash in the direction of Rob's pudgy hobbit feet.

I hate his feet.

He has fat dirt stained toes and calloused skin from walking around the house barefoot. What I hated most though was that at some point throughout the night they'd end up in my lap, and that man would whine like a two year old until I touched them.

Looking at Rob's yellow-tinged nail beds, I'd say they're just as gross as they used to be.

At least he's wearing shoes today.

I realize these are old feelings clawing their way out of the basement. I need to find some new ones if we're to make it through this weekend… like impassiveness. Rob and I should be able to be in the same room together because I don't care about him. I've moved on with my life. I don't need to worry about him or his toes or anything else I used to stress over.

"Can we talk?" Rob sticks his hand in his pockets and makes his best attempt to look innocent, like the boy I met right out of college. Not that he was innocent back then. That man had more life experience than most adults twice his age, but in comparison he was. "Alone."

"No." Noah answers for me. It's the kind of *no* a dad says to a kid at Walmart throwing a fit over a toy. Strong, with no room for argument.

I love him for jumping in and trying to be my rock, but Rob and I probably should talk. We have two miserable days together and we *need* to be civil, for Ethan and Gemma's sake. If I put our conversation off, Rob will corner me every chance he gets. I might as well get this over with now.

"Five minute is all you get," I say to Rob then nudge Noah's arm and smile up at him. "I'll be okay."

I'm not sure I believe what I'm saying, but to my credit I sound half convincing. At least I think I do.

"I'm watching you," Noah warns Rob. Thankfully after that weird show of… whatever that was… Noah gives me a soft smile and leaves.

"I'm just over there," I say to Noah when Rob begins to walk away. "I've got this."

My stomach twists the further Noah gets. He sits on the edge of an empty lounge chair, elbows resting on his knees and tilts his chin up at me. I nod slightly, reading into the unspoken encouragement. I've been doing that a lot today. Finding words that don't exist. This time I find *You can do this* in Noah's gaze. It's what I needed to hear—or not hear, I guess—to muster the courage to turn around and meet my ex at the diving board.

"You look good, Harper. I like what you've done with yourself." Rob pauses, eyes trailing over my body again.

"What do you want, Rob?" My instincts are at war with each other. Half of me wants to see what he has to say while the other half wants to run. I'm not worried about falling into his bed again. The ship where I found him attractive has long sailed.

It's the thoughts that will creep up tonight. Memories I think I've moved past. There's a chance it'll be too much to bear and that fear is what has one foot of mine out the door and back into my rental car. But running gives Rob power, and I refuse to be seen as weak again.

"Baby girl." Rob reaches for my elbow. His touch catches me off guard. He pulls me into his chest and wraps his arms around my waist. I'm hit with the familiar scent of cherry Black and Mild cigars and weed. "I don't like the way we left things. What do you say we try again and end things right?"

"Excuse me?" I arch back and shake my head.

"Come on, baby." Rob tries to close the space between us. He puckers his lips and leans in.

I don't move. I can't, I'm in shock. I don't know whether to feel flattered or insulted. Rob didn't ask how I've been. He didn't want to know if I'm single, with a boyfriend, or married. He just assumed that whatever my relationship status was I'd cheat for him. I'd throw everything I've worked for away…for him!

Something hooks the belt loops on each side of my hips and pulls me backward, out of Rob's hold. My back presses against a firm chest as an arm protectively wraps around my belly. I tense not sure as to what's happening, then relax when I smell the caramel scent of Noah's cologne. *I guess my five minutes are up.*

"You good, babe?" Noah asks, cheerfully, his lips close to my ear.

"Babe?" Rob arches one bushy eyebrow. He laughs until Noah wraps his other arm around me. His face falls as the little gears in his head start turning. "Is there something going on I should know about?"

This is the moment I fuck up. I realize it the second my words are out of my mouth. Before thinking about the consequences, or even what the answer to that question should be, I say, "Not that it's any of your business, but yes. Noah and I are dating."

"Bullshit," Rob bites out. He grits his teeth together, flexing the muscles over his cheeks.

Sweet satisfaction has me fighting a smile. I hope Rob is thinking about all the times I said there was no reason to worry about Noah. I defended our friendship daily because Rob hated how much time we spent together. Back then Noah and I were *just* friends. Now, we're somewhere between strangers with history and acquaintances.

But no one needs to know how far I pushed Noah away this year.

A blanket of red coats Rob's cheeks down to his thick neck. Noah holds me tighter against him, probably worried that Rob will make a scene. "Noah's been friend-zoned. There's no coming back from that."

Noah *was* friend-zoned my freshman year of college... sort of... and things between us only became even more platonic as time went on. Rob knows this, just like I know he doubted Noah and I were *just* friends.

I don't give Noah a warning as to what I'm going to do, and in thinking about it, this could have gone horribly wrong. If it had I probably would have tucked my tail and disappeared, but I don't give myself time to second guess my decision.

I turn and loop my arms around Noah's neck. My fingers brush against his nape, finally touching those curls I've been itching to play with since I set eyes on them. Noah liked to keep his hair short. I haven't seen it this long since we were in middle school.

I send a silent plea into the universe and hope Noah is still able to read me. I hesitate for half of a heart beat, just long enough for him to pull away. That moment passes, so I grab Noah by the shirt collar and press his lips to mine. His mouth is soft and hard at the same time. Welcoming, yet standoffish. A low growl, deep in his throat, escapes as I swipe my tongue across the seam of his lips.

He lets me in and every thought, every fear I've had about this weekend vanishes. I step forward and Noah takes a step back. He lets me take the lead, gauging what I'm comfortable with while his hands roam my body. I laugh against his lips as we bump into one of the outstretched lounge chairs. Noah falls onto it, bringing me down with him. I spread my legs over his lap and close my eyes, enjoying the rollercoaster of emotions running through me.

This is surreal.

A squeal from somewhere around us jerks me out of the moment. I pull back, exhaling a heavy breath and lean my forehead against Noah's. I don't know what this is, or what these feelings mean, but I don't have the time to figure it out because Gemma has found us.

I wince at the high pitched shrill she emits, but smile. Gemma stares at us, bouncing on her toes, then squeals again. "No. Freaking. Way!"

I slide off of Noah's lap and squint in the direction of the female battle cry. I've never been a screamer—unless it was in bed—but this sound is second to breathing in Gemma's world.

She lunges the moment my ass hits the plastic bands of the beach chair. Her arms wrap around my shoulders and she shoves us both against Noah. He takes us in stride, used to our shenanigans.

Or what used to be our shenanigans.

"You're here! And this…" Gemma finally lets me go and hops over to the beach chair beside us. "When did you two become an item?"

Rob clears his throat. I had forgotten he was standing beside us, and kind of hoped that our little PDA show had chased him away. No such luck. "That's exactly what I want to know."

Chapter 3

NOAH

IN ALL THE years we've been friends, throughout all the awkward situations she's put me in, Harper Richards has never pretended I was her boyfriend.

Not once.

But, hell. I'll run with it. If Harper wants me to be her boyfriend, then I'm going to be the best damn boyfriend she's ever had, real or fake.

I wrap my arms around her waist and pull her against me. Soft edges mold into my hard frame. She leans against me like we used to when we were kids, and I'm taken back to high school; to when we thought having different homerooms was the end of the world.

"I don't know, babe." I rest my chin on Harper's shoulder. I know this is all for show, to keep Rob off her back this weekend, but that doesn't mean I'm not going to have some fun in the process. This is a chance I never thought I'd have again. Why not milk it for everything it's worth? "We never had an official *lets date* moment, but we were a long time coming. How long would you say we've been at it?"

Harper strokes my arm and my mind goes somewhere it shouldn't. "About a year. Everything before that doesn't count because we weren't sleeping together."

Rob chokes and sprays his beer on the deck. "A fucking year?"

"I knew it." Gemma beams.

She's still got that new mom glow, even though her son, Preston, is almost two now. Only, that glow radiates into everything she does because Gemma is… well, Gemma.

"I mean, I didn't know you and Harper had gotten together, but I figured there was something besides work keeping you away all this time. I was hoping you'd found someone." Gemma turns her gaze from me to reach out and squeeze Harper's arm. "I'm so glad it's you."

Harper stiffens under my touch. We may have drifted apart, but she's still the girl I fell in love with in the eighth grade. The same girl who prays for road kill and buys an extra cheeseburger at McDonald's just in case there's a homeless person on the corner. The girl who cried while watching *The Fox and the Hound* and was pissed when Elena switched to team Damon. I know her. I know this lie is eating away at her and at some point, everything is going to come crashing down. When it does, I'll be there to pick up the pieces.

I always am.

"Won't Ethan be looking for you?" Harper stands and smooths the wrinkles from her shirt. She looks back and flashes me a smile. It's fake, like the ones she'd put on at Rob's parties, that don't reach her eyes. Another act for our little show. "We should probably head over to the reception area before he thinks you've run off."

Gemma rolls her big green eyes and links her arm through Harper's. "That man knows I'm not going anywhere. You, on the other hand, we can't say that about."

I hang back, letting the girls have some privacy to catch up. Rob swings to the left of the deck and finds the date he brought. I never liked that man, and hated every minute Harper was with him. Even though their breakup was unexpected and nearly cost Harper her life, I'm glad she overdosed that night. It was the push she needed to get away from him.

I make my way to the bar and order a Coke this time, no liquor. I need a clear head to pull whatever this is off. I know myself and one drink will turn into two, which will end up closer to four or five, and then I'll be stumbling down the minefield that is memory lane.

Seeing Harper is hard enough. Holding her, kissing her like she's mine this weekend and then watching her walk away will destroy me. I can handle it sober. Not like this is the first time. But drunk… there's no telling what truths I might spill.

A different bartender than the one we had earlier sets my drink on a napkin-square. I pull the lighter out of my pocket and flick the spinner. I carry it out of habit, even though I haven't smoked in years. I stopped doing a lot of things after Harper's overdose. Seemed like the best decision at the time.

Back then, I quit drinking.

Quit smoking.

Pulled away from our friends.

Bought a condo and moved out of town.

I did everything I thought would be best for Harper after she got out of rehab, because I was counting on her coming back to me. She was my best friend. More than a best friend. I can't say she was like a sister, because we'd slept together back in high school, but our bond was family-strong.

Or so I thought.

After about thirty minutes of being Gemma's personal show pony, Harper breaks away. I'm proud of her. She lasted longer than I expected. She slumps onto the stool next to me and grabs my drink. Without hesitation, she tips it back, gulping what's left in two big swallows.

She sets my empty cup down with an audible exhale and drops her head back. "My cheeks hurt. I can't remember the last time I smiled so much."

"How'd you know there wasn't alcohol in that?" I watch her, waiting for some physical reaction to signal she's fallen off the wagon. It's hard to judge someone's actions through a few measly text messages, but Harper seemed to be doing well and I never doubted her.

Now, though, I'm worried.

Harper lifts her head. She's not glaring, but she's not smiling either. Her face is a blank canvas and I feel like shit for wondering, but I can't help it. I worry about her. *I always worry about her.*

"Your cup was plastic. Bars don't put whiskey or whatever in plastic cups."

"Some places do."

She reaches for my hand, letting her fingers link with mine. Her hand is warm. Soft. Her fingers barely reach my knuckles and yet they interlace with mine like they're made to be together. "I'm good, Noah. I promise. If your cup had something in it, I would have ruined your drink and spit it all back inside."

"I won't drink around you this weekend. It was a mistake to have that one earlier."

"Noah." Harper scoots to the edge of the stool and takes my other hand in hers. She faces me, dark brown eyes locked onto mine. "You don't have to do that. I'm stronger than you think."

She might be, but am I? "What's the plan, Har? How far are we taking this fake-dating-thing this weekend?"

Harper drops my hands and reaches for the pack of smokes in her boot. She's gone through all but three of her cigarettes. At this rate, she's going to leave on Sunday with lung cancer. I get it though, she feels like she needs *something* when things get tough.

I blow her match out. She doesn't need the crutch, she's got me.

Harper sighs but nods, seeming to understand that her smoking is getting out of control. She sets the unlit cigarette on the bar top, then shrugs. "I'm sorry, Noah. I panicked. Is there a woman in your life I need to apologize to?"

I almost laugh. I've had a few one night stands, but there hasn't been anyone I've wanted to keep. Sometimes the girls would sleep over, and I'd wake with them in my arms, but they never felt right. The only girl I've ever wanted was Harper and none of the others could compare. "Nope, just me. We can do whatever you need to to sell the story."

"I don't know, Noah." She chews on the corner of her lip.

"I told you, whatever you need." I reach up and thread my fingers through her hair. I bring her face close enough to kiss. I crave those lips, but there's no one around. No reason she could justify me taking what I want. Instead I whisper in her ear, "I've got your back."

"There you are!" Gemma runs up to us with Ethan, his parents, and their son, Preston, in tow. "I should have known you'd sneak off to find Noah. Preston is dying to build sand castles, so we're getting changed and heading down to the beach. You two should come."

"I... um... we..." Harper looks torn. She looks up at me for guidance and if the woman thinks I'm going to miss out on seeing her in a bathing suit she's got another thing coming.

"That sounds great." I drape one arm over Harper's shoulder. Her pulse is beating like an angry monster beneath her skin. I can feel it on the crook of my arm, that fragile heart begging to be saved. "We'll meet you down there in about a half hour."

"Great! I'll see you there." Gemma turns and swoops Preston into her arms. He laughs the way kids do, with their whole hearts, and full of expression. Ethan stops as he walks by to shake my hand, but doesn't stay to chat. I get it. The next three days are going to be a whirlwind of craziness. He hurries after his bride-to-be and son, leaving Harper and I alone again.

"I don't have a bathing suit," Harper says once they're out of earshot. Her neck is red, a telltale sign of another panic attack looming in the distance. When we dated, I never knew Harper had anxiety issues. She was outgoing and put together. It wasn't until she got together with Rob that I witnessed her first episode. Scared the living hell out of me. They've been a problem for her ever since.

"Let me guess, your plan was to hide in your room most of the weekend?" She shrugs, and I can't help but smile.

"It's a good thing you have a doting boyfriend who likes to splurge on his one true love."

"No." She shakes her head. "These beach shops are just as bad as theme parks. A twenty dollar shirt will cost an arm and a leg. I can't begin to imagine how much a bathing suit will cost."

I take Harper's hand and guide her off the stool. I like holding it, feeling her warm skin on mine. I don't know what she does for a living, but I can imagine spending a hundred dollars on a bathing suit isn't in her budget.

As for me, my house in Palm Beach pays for itself and my current mortgage. My job lets me work as many hours as I want. No one wants to be on-call and I take every shift offered because, unlike my co-workers, I don't have a family at home.

I smirk and lead us into the gift shop. They have a selection of skimpy two-pieces on the back wall that Harper would look amazing in. They also have a few modest one pieces that I'll happily buy if that's what she prefers. Not gonna lie though, I'd love to see Harper in a bikini again. "Then I guess we'd better get my money's worth."

Chapter 4

HARPER

NOTHING.

There is nothing I can afford in this overpriced, tourist trap, gift shop. I lift the tag of the only one-piece bathing suit in my size—a white, strappy, cut-out that has as much fabric as a bikini—feeling my stomach drop to my feet. "Two hundred and fifty dollars. This is insane. I should just wear shorts and a shirt."

"And let Rob shove his current piece of ass in your face? Hell, no." Noah holds up a royal blue bikini that has chunky straps. The bottom has a small cut out of a heart on the front. It's cute, but not wearable with the four day stubble I've got going on.

I shake my head and stride over to the clearance rack. Forty percent off of an eighty dollar bikini top is outrageous, but at least it's something. Too bad everything I've found so far is either hideous or huge, but maybe I missed something. I thumb through each item on the rack for a third time, not looking at the prices this go around but the size. "I take it you're talking about Jessica Rabbit?"

Noah puts on a pair of not-so-cheap, should-be-dollar-store glasses and checks himself out in the mirror. Deja vous slaps me in the face and I realize we've done this before, back when we were in high school. One of our Friday night must-do's consisted of going into a surf shop, without a dollar in our pockets, and trying on everything we wanted but couldn't afford.

Noah puts the red pair of shades back on the rack and tries on a pair of black ones. "Who?"

I push through the fog that is our past and focus on the task at hand:

finding a bathing suit and figuring out how to describe Rob's date without sounding like a jealous psycho. "Red hair. Big boobs. Skin tight, black dress." I'm tempted to add that Rob was trying to eat her face every time I looked at him, but that would imply I was watching them...and that I care...which I don't. "Jessica Rabbit. She's even got the goofy, big eared, hairy lover at her side."

"Oh, shit! You're right. That fits them perfectly." Noah laughs and the sound warms my soul. It's been a long time since I heard him so carefree. It makes me miss the nights where we'd hang out by the fire and talk about nothing for hours. Or, if I go back further, I miss sitting on the bleachers watching him play basketball, getting ice cream after, and our walks along the beach.

I close my eyes, surprised at the hole I made in my heart by pushing Noah away this year. Each memory is a double edged sword and no matter which side I touch, it cuts me. I miss who I used to be. If I could, I'd go back to those days and hold onto what we had and to who I could have been.

The sting of tears burns my eyes and nose. I promised myself I wouldn't cry this weekend. Clearly, I'm not going to keep my promise. The least I can do is hold on to my shred of dignity and not be seen. I grab the first swimsuit I touch and turn toward the dressing rooms. "I think I want to try this one on."

"That one?" Noah asks, amusement dancing in his tone.

I open my eyes and look down at the pink and gray pho-camo set of strings I grabbed. Even if I wanted to wear them—which I don't—they're four sizes too big. I force a laugh and set it back on the rack.

There's a display beach chair in the corner of the room, surrounded by sand toys. I collapse into it and drop my face into my hands. At this rate, I'm never going to find something to wear, let alone make it through the weekend.

I feel too much.

"Harper?"

I lift my head, too exhausted to fight the tears pooling behind my eyes. Noah's got two white bags in his hand, but drops them on the ground when he sees me. I must look as bad as I feel because he rushes to my side, falls to his knees, and wraps his arms around me.

It feels good to be held, which only makes me feel worse because I am not this person.

I don't need someone to hold my hand and tell me everything is going to be all right and Noah shouldn't be fighting my battles. I should be able to stand in front of Rob, a proud, single woman, and let his bullshit roll off my back but I can't.

The ghosts of my past haunt me even though I'm not an addict anymore. They're here, poking at my resolve, begging me to give in and have just one drink or open the pills my therapist prescribed. They want me to relapse and I'm trying so hard to keep my shit together, but I don't have the money for a new bathing suit and this feels like the straw that's going to break me.

I give into the bottomless feeling and let myself cry into Noah's shoulder. Tears are good for the soul. They lift the weight of life and temporarily send my ghosts back to the hell they crawled out of. I used to think bawling my eyes out made me weak, but my therapist taught me that it's the opposite. It takes a brave woman to give into her emotions. People hide behind what they don't want to deal with by using drugs, drinking, or even through sex.

I don't hide behind my vices anymore.

I face them, head on, which is why I'm not afraid to admit I'm scared and overwhelmed, and confused. God, I'm so confused. I don't know what this is that I'm feeling toward Noah. Fake dating this weekend might just be the worst decision I've made all year.

Noah lifts my head into his hands and swipes his thumbs across my cheeks. He looks me in the eyes, without a shred of judgment. "Remember, Starlight, you are beautiful, and strong, and whatever it is you're fighting... you are not alone. I'll be by your side every step of the way."

"Starlight?"

"You won't let me call you princess anymore." He shrugs and leans forward, stopping a breath away from my mouth. Waiting for me to make the next move.

There must be someone from the wedding party in the shop I didn't notice, because why else would Noah want to kiss me?

We've known each other our whole lives and I've been in the friend-zone for almost half of it. He never once made a move after we broke up. Not when I moved back to Florida for college or in any of the million breakups

Rob and I had. If he's this close, it's because he doesn't want to blow our cover.

So, even though I'm a blubbering, snotty mess, I tilt my chin and invite him in. This time, Noah doesn't devour me. He doesn't pull my body against his and sear me with his touch. He doesn't send my heart soaring or make my head swim with lust.

What Noah does to me in the beach-toy section of the gift shop is far worse than anything I experienced outside.

He makes me feel.

His fingers slide into my hair, awakening every nerve in my body. Pinpoints of electricity shoot down my spine to my toes. They spread through my body until I feel every hair stand on edge.

He traces the seam of my lips, waiting for me to open my mouth. The tiny voice in the back of my head says this is a bad idea. It reminds me that in two days we'll be distant friends again, but I don't care.

I give in because as wrong as it is, I don't want this feeling to stop.

The way Noah moves his tongue is unlike anything I've ever experienced. It's like he's trying to absorb every inch of me, every move I make against him, and commit it to memory.

This is a kiss of goodbye, which is confusing as hell because we still have two days together. The kind of kiss someone who just had their heart broken would give. One where there's years of pain and suffering behind it, but also love. The kind of love you let go of to ensure your partner's happiness.

I pull back, drowning in a new sea of emotions because, *what was that?*

Noah sits on his heels again. His lips lift into a sad smile that matches everything I felt. "I know we're supposed to meet Gemma soon, but would you want to go for a walk on the beach? For old time's sake?"

"Yeah. That would be fun."

Chapter 5

HARPER

CREAMY, white, liquid drips down my arm.

I lick it, fighting a losing battle with the Florida heat. My ice cream melts quicker than I can eat as Noah and I walk the paper white shore. I slurp the milkshake inside my cone, trying my hardest not to become any more of a sticky mess, but it's useless.

Noah shakes his head, laughing at my futile attempt to stay clean. He walks along the water's edge, letting the salt water wash over his toes. "I warned you not to get the extra-large waffle cone."

I hold my ice cream out, hoping he'll take a lick or two. Or ten. Even if I were to take giant sized bites, there is no way I can finish this by myself. There's too much of everything.

"Nu-uh. I already ate mine. Besides, Cookie Dough is the worst."

He did not just say what I think he said! I gasp, stopping in my tracks. "Take it back."

Noah grins, knowing my love for all things cookie. If I could, I'd eat them all day long. Chocolate chip is my favorite, especially if they come from Publix, but I'm not picky. I eat them all: sugar, Oreo, peanut butter, heath bar crunch… you name it and I've tried it at least once. Also, I know for a fact that Noah's least favorite ice cream is lemon sherbert and that he has, on more than one occasion, helped me polish off a carton of cookie dough in front of a sappy chick-flick.

"Now, Rocky Road, that's a flavor I can get behind. If you'd gotten that one I might be willing to eat an extra scoop." Noah pats his flat stomach, looking pensive. "Cookie dough though..." He sticks his tongue out, making a *yuck* expression, and shakes his head.

I throw the soup that used to be my ice cream and hit him in the chest. I set my hands on my hips and arch my eyebrows. He should know better than to hate on the best flavor in the world, especially when it's covered in chocolate fudge and gummy bears.

Noah pulls the ice cream stained shirt over his head and tosses it in the sand. I stand there, practically salivating at how much his body has changed. He always had comfort weight on his belly, but there was never enough for him to be called fat, and I distinctly remember him having that indent by his hips men get when they work out, along with the faint lines of a six-pack.

But damn. Noah must live at the gym these days because there isn't an inch of extra anything on him. His chest is firm, his abs defined. The hair that went from his pecks to below his belt is gone. There's nothing but golden, silky, skin staring at me, begging to be licked.

He chuckles, drawing my gaze back to his face. I shrug, unashamed to be caught checking him out. I've caught his eyes skimming over my curves in the cutout one-piece he bought me.

We stand there, in a stare off, until his eyes narrow. I recognize the devious look in them, and realize I'm fucked.

I drop my flip flops, and turn, running as fast as I can toward the hotel stairs. Gemma wasn't down here when Noah and I got to the beach earlier, but we've been walking for a while. If I can find and get to her, maybe I can avoid whatever revenge Noah's got planned.

The soft sand flies out from under my feet, putting distance between us, but it's not enough. Noah's arms wrap around my waist and he lifts me into the air. I scream as he carries me toward the water.

Even though the white one piece he picked out is made for just this, it's white!

White is see through!

In the ten minutes I had to get ready, I was able to trim my bikini line and (thankfully) didn't have a full carpet growing down below, but it would be my luck that the fabric would be defective and everyone on the beach would see the color difference and *know* I'm not waxed.

Or worse...

My nipples.

My girls are far from huge, but these C-cups need support! They need more padding than this barely lined top offers. Most importantly, they need to not be seen!

I kick my legs, trying to free myself, but Noah has a death grip on me. He runs knee deep into the water and hurls me into a wave like a frisbee. I gulp in a breath of air just before breaking through the surface. Going under feels like a million needles pricking my body. The ocean colder than I expect, but once my skin adjusts to the temperature change, it feels amazing.

I find my footing as a baby wave crashes against my back. I push my hair off my face and flick lingering water droplets off my hands. I wipe my thumb under my eyes, expecting to find eyeliner and mascara smudges. Thankfully, my makeup is holding up.

"You're so dead." I run to Noah, although running in water is more like a slow motion camera effect. I either have to high-knee it or push through the resistance. I choose the latter. I may not be trying to impress anyone, but I'm also not trying to look like an uncoordinated spaz either.

Another wave hits me from behind and knocks me to my knees. My palm lands on something sharp, sending a surge of pain up my hand and into my arm. I must make a face because Noah is at my side, high-knee running, not caring how ridiculous he looks.

He grabs me by my elbows and lifts me to my feet. "Are you okay?"

"Yeah, but I think I hit my hand on something."

"Let me see."

I lift my hand as another wave pushes me into his chest. Strong arms wrap around my waist, holding me so I won't fall again. I look up into his eyes. The usually bright green irises are dark, almost the hue of his pupils.

Noah's fingers caress my lower back. His touch burns my skin in ways the cool water can't quench.

This is bad.

I want him, even though I shouldn't. Even though I know I'm going to get hurt. I should put a stop to this now, before I do something that will ruin the tattered friendship we have.

Logically, I recognize I'm deflecting my issues with Rob and clinging to Noah. Just like I know if we keep this up, I'm going to leave confused and probably regretting every minute of what we're doing, but I don't care.

I want to feel Noah's lips on mine. I want to know if he's going to suck me down that emotional vortex again or if he's going to set my body on fire. "You know you want to kiss me."

Noah brushes his thumb against my bottom lip, reminding me what it's like to feel him. "Why would you say that?"

"Because you're my fake boyfriend." And I want you to want me.

Another wave crashes into us, closing what little space there was between our bodies, but Noah doesn't make a move. He just stares at my mouth, lost in his own thoughts.

I wait, and wish, and hope he will lean down to kiss me, but as seconds turn into minutes I realize he's not going to. Without an audience, Noah has no reason to want me.

I look away, unable to take the tension any longer. My gaze flicks over to the shore. Gemma sets up a blanket and umbrella while trying to keep little Preston out of the sun's harsh rays. "Gemma just came out to the beach. I'm sure everyone will be following her shortly."

Noah grunts and takes a step back. I hate the distance between us. I shiver and miss his touch as soon as it's gone, but it's clear he isn't going to pull me into his arms again, or take my hand.

He turns and makes his way to the shore, then sits just outside of the tide's reach. We're less than a foot apart but I feel the divide, a shift I'm creating that makes me second guess every selfish motivation I have about keeping our charade going.

"What's wrong, Noah?" I ask, sitting beside him.

He digs his fingers into the sand, creating tiny mountains that he destroys like an angry giant. Those ever-changing greens betray him, showcasing a hurt I assume has something to do with our arrangement. "I don't know, Harper. This is…"

"This is what?" I cut him off because I'm scared of what Noah will say.

A bad idea? Yeah, I agree.

A mistake? Probably. But knowing the truth and hearing Noah say it are two different things. Having the words run through my mind, I can pass them off as irrational insecurity and convince myself that our friendship is strong enough to handle something like this.

Hearing him say those things… well that would make reality set in and I want to keep living this dream with him, just for a little while longer.

Noah shakes his head and leans back onto the sand, tucking one arm behind his head. "Never mind. I know I said I'll do whatever you need this weekend, but we should probably set some ground rules. Things we aren't cool with."

"That's a good idea. I'm not a fan of oral," I blurt without thinking. *Please tell me I didn't say that out loud.*

Noah's mouth falls open. "Wow. I...uh...okay."

My face burns red. Can I take that back? Maybe bury my head in the sand and disappear? Nope, bad idea. That would have me on my knees, ass up in the air and now I'm picturing Noah behind me with his hands on my hips, slamming into me while his nuts hit my clit.

Fuck me. That's an image.

I'm not cold anymore. I'm hot everywhere and I don't think it has anything to do with the Florida sun.

"I'm just saying." I tuck my hair behind my ears. I hope they're not as red as I feel. All I need is for Noah to ask me what's on my mind and read between the lines of my *nothing*. "I... um... I'm not a fan of being gone down on. I don't mind giving head though."

"That's a shame, Starlight."

"Why's that?"

"Because my tongue is almost as skilled as my dick."

I choke on nothing but the thought. Noah grins at my embarrassment which sinks the knife deeper. We've talked about sex before, but not in relation to doing things with each other. That ship sailed years ago. "That's... um...wonderful?"

"What's your favorite position, woman I'm supposed to be in with?"

I meet his gaze again, mortified. Turned on. And hella confused. "Is that really necessary?"

"You're the one who said we needed to be prepared for anything." Noah smiles with a closed mouth smile.

I have a feeling he's enjoying this more than he should. The question is, why? Is he genuinely curious? Trying to be a good fake boyfriend? Or does he like making me blush?

"What if Rob starts asking questions about our sex life?" he adds to beef up the argument.

I raise my brow at him. "Seriously, why would he do that?"

"Because Rob is a twisted, jealous man. Mark my words, he will throw something from your past in my face and I will need to come back with a story of my own. If there isn't at least one detail he can recognize, I'll be called on my bluff and this shit will go sideways."

I gotta hand it to him, Noah's argument is sound. That one hundred percent is something Rob would do.

I stare at Noah and try to remember what sex with him was like. We didn't know what we were doing back in high school. We were probably missionary folks back then, but I'd like to think it was good. Nothing jumps out at me as a bad experience, so that counts. Unfortunately, the more I try to remember, the less I can recall. Outside of knowing that we've slept together, those memories are long gone.

My cheeks flush, wondering what tricks he's picked up over the years. I know I've learned a few he'd probably like. "Fine. On my back. Knees up by your chest."

"See. That wasn't so bad." Noah grabs a handful of sand and lets the grains slip from his grasp, building a small, dribble castle between us. He looks bored and for some reason that irks me. Sex with me is not boring. I've never had a man complain or struggle to come. I have a grade-A pussy and he needs to know this!

"With your hand around my neck." Or a gag in my mouth. A little bit of bondage is always fun. Oh! Definitely a finger pressed against, if not in, my ass too. I bite my lip. Images of him satisfying me flicker through my mind. We'd have fun together, because I know Noah likes it rough, but I doubt our fake relationship will bring us anywhere near the bedroom.

Noah chuckles and shoots me a sideways glance. "Kinky."

I roll onto my side and prop my head in my hand. My nipples pucker beneath the thin white fabric that may hide the color of my areolas but damn sure doesn't cover my arousal. Noah's eyes drop to my chest again and this time I catch him looking. *Is he thinking about fucking me, like I am him, too?* "Your turn."

Noah pushes onto his elbows and stares at me. The way his gaze slithers into my soul makes me shudder. He could always see beneath the walls I built, tell with one look if something was wrong. The question is, can he tell I want to rip his shorts off and see if he's as turned on as I am?

Noah doesn't respond and his lack of answer makes the hairs on the back of my neck stand. *Can* he tell? I feel nauseous, nervous that he doesn't want me too. Why would he? I'm damaged goods.

Used and abused.

Rob's sloppy seconds.

Noah's pity reruns.

I'm like the book everyone keeps on the shelf that's already been read. Liked enough not to donate, pretty to look at, but we all know deep down it's never going to be opened again.

I can't take it anymore. I crack, but try to sound like I'm not freaking out when I ask, "What?"

"Your boob is about to pop out."

"What?" I look down and frown. My left girl is hanging on by the ball of my nipple ring. I sit upright and tuck her back into place. Fucking hell. This is why itty bitty bathing suits aren't for me. I laugh both frustrated and relieved. "Thanks."

"A good boyfriend would be encouraging you to sunbathe naked," he adds with a shit eating grin.

It's hard not to match it when I want to strangle and kiss the man at the same time. There's a reason why Noah and I are better off as friends. We would drive each other to madness if we were actually together, and I'd probably be pregnant within a week. I need to remember that, and that this is fake.

Noah isn't my boyfriend. He's just a guy I know, doing me a solid.

If he wanted me, even as a one-time-fun-fuck, he would have made his move a long time ago. And yet I can't resist having a little fun.

"A better boyfriend would have saved me from a wardrobe malfunction by copping a feel and then kissing me." I meet Noah's gaze, staring intensely, challenging him to make a move. With Gemma only a few dozen feet away, acting on my urges is easy, I can blame it all on our pretend relationship.

Noah's throat bobs with a swallow. Our bodies inch closer at a painfully slow speed. I tilt my chin, giving him a silent invitation and part my lips. His head dips, lips hovering just above mine. I want this more than I should. The gift shop left me hungry. I need to know if that was a kiss of goodbye or if it held deeper emotion. More importantly, I need to know if I'm overthinking things because my mind is running in too many circles.

"Hey, love birds!" Gemma yells, jogging up to us. I fight a groan with a smile and look up at my other used-to-be-bestie. "Hate to interrupt, but Ethan needs you on his team, Noah. Apparently, it's life or death."

"Gotta run." Noah hops to his feet and sprints across the beach.

I haven't seen him move that fast since he was on the football team. It stings, and the painful thought that he's eager to get away from me adds another dime to my insecurity jar. He high fives Ethan, then gets ready for... I don't know what. Ultimate frisbee? Is that still a thing?

"Don't be mad, but I've gotta know..." Gemma sits next to me, crossing her legs and making a visor with her hand.

I turn my attention back to Gemma. Her fair skin isn't meant for the Florida sun. She tries to hide it with leggings, a long sleeved swim shirt, and an oversized hat, but her hands and cheeks are already starting to burn and she's been outside for less than ten minutes.

"Why didn't you tell me about you and Noah?"

"Yeah..." Jessica Rabbit interjects. She towers above us, hands on her hips. I don't know where she came from, but I wish she'd go back down the hole she wiggled out of. "Why didn't you tell your *best friend* you and Noah were dating?"

I twist to look over my shoulder. This woman is getting on my nerves. First with her C-rated, PG-13 porn on the pool deck; and now she's butting into my business. "Who are you? And why are you in this conversation?"

"I came to warn you." She sets her manicured fingers on her hips and glares. "Stay away from Rob."

I laugh, a full on, belly roll laugh. The whole reason Noah and I are in this situation is to keep Rob away from me. The fact that this chick is marking her territory tells me my ex hasn't changed a bit. I feel sorry for her. She has no idea the roller coaster of hell she's in for with that man.

"Trust me, you've got nothing to worry about." Because I'd rather stab myself in the eye with the dull end of a stick than touch Rob again. "Noah keeps me more than satisfied."

"Eeeek!" Gemma squeals, clapping her hands. "This all makes sense! Noah didn't want to be Ethan's best man because he wanted to walk down the aisle with you. He's such a sweetheart."

"What are you talking about?" Jessica Rabbit scoffs. "Rob is the best man."

"Only because Noah said no." Gemma covers her mouth with her hands as soon as the words are out. "Oh, my gosh. I wasn't supposed to say anything. Lydia, you can't tell Rob. He was so excited when Ethan asked."

Lydia lifts her lips into a crooked grin. "Don't worry. I've got your back, Gems. Unlike this one." She walks down to the water's edge and then over to the boys.

"What's she talking about?" I've answered every phone call, replied to every text Gemma has ever sent. She's never asked me to come home, not until now, but if she had, I would have. She knows this. I even offered to come back for Preston's birthday last year and she told me no.

Gemma forces a smile and stands. "Oh, that's just Lydia. Stirring up drama." She brushes the sand off her legs then adjusts her hat. "I'm cooking, though. If I don't get under the umbrella soon, Ethan's gonna have a lobster at the altar tomorrow, not a bride. You coming?"

Something about the way Gemma deflected doesn't feel right. The longer I look at her, the more I see it. A smile that doesn't reach her eyes. The faint hue of dark circles hidden beneath the concealer. The signs everyone saw on me when I was drowning, but ignored.

"What's going on Gem? Are you having second thoughts about getting married?"

"What? No!" Gemma laughs, and I catch it again. The hint of sadness behind the mask. "I've just been down a lot lately. Having a hard time shaking the post-partum blues, but I'm good. I promise."

"Gem." I stand and throw my arms around her. "Why didn't you tell me?"

She pulls back, fixes her hat, and shrugs like struggling is no big deal, but she's wrong. Mental health is everything. It can take the strongest person and break them. It's the unseen knife gutting people in front of a crowd. I should know. I've felt its blade hacking away when people were looking me dead in the eye. If anyone can understand not being okay, it's me.

"You had a lot going on. I didn't want to add anything more to your plate."

I rest my hands on her shoulders. Gemma has been my rock throughout my rebuilding process, the voice in my ear telling me to keep going. The only person I let know I needed help after I left because I knew she wouldn't pass judgment. I couldn't have done it without her in my corner.

I feel terrible for not coming home sooner.

She should have told me.

"That's no excuse. You're my best friend." As far as friends go, she's been amazing whereas I have been shit. Clearly. I didn't know she was depressed and we talk daily. *God, I suck.*

"And you're mine." Gemma glances over at the guys. They're running around, like a bunch of kids, chasing a plastic disc. The look on Noah's face is murderous. I don't remember how the boys keep score, but I'd wager that Rob and Cash—Gemma's step-brother—are winning. "But don't tell Ethan. He's already sour you stole Noah away. Lord only knows what kind of man-fit he'll throw if he thinks you're taking me too."

We both stand and wipe the sand off our asses. I link arms with her and lean my head on her shoulder, hoping that she'll understand I'm always going to be here for her. Just because I've got shit going on in my life doesn't mean I can't be there for her too. "Your secret is safe with me."

Chapter 6

HARPER

I COVER my face with my arm, trying to block the sun's rays. The boys have been playing frisbee for almost two hours, and I'm ready to go. My skin is borderline burnt and the cooler is officially out of everything non-alcoholic. As tempting as that rabbit hole may be, I'm not falling down it.

"Little man's getting sleepy," Gemma says aloud to whoever is listening. Preston's curled up in her lap, his thumb in his mouth. She rocks him, frowning at the guys. "They'll be at this for hours if we don't put a stop to it." She bites the inside of her cheek, then looks at me. "Do you mind being the big bad witch and telling Ethan it's time to go?"

"Of course." I sit upright, proud that she asked me and not Jessica Rabbit to do the deed. I'm met with a solid eye roll from Ms. Rabbit which makes me even happier. *That's right, bitch. Still number one.* "I'm ready to go too. Mind if I walk up with you?"

"Sure." Gemma smiles and rubs circles on Preston's back. "Are you and Noah staying in the same room?"

Shit. I'd forgotten about that bit. If Jessica Rabbit—I mean Lydia—wasn't here, I'd tell Gemma a half-truth. That I had booked a room too, not realizing Noah had already taken care of things. I'd tell her it was too late to cancel, so I was staying down on the third floor while Noah would be on the eighth with the rest of the wedding party.

But Lydia is staring, with her pencil thin eyebrows arched, looking for ammo to use against me.

"Yeah." I stand and brush the sand off the back of my thighs. *Fuck. Fuck. Fuck!* "I've gotta get the room key from him. I'll be right back."

The sun beats down on the sand, reflecting beams of white light. I squint against the brightness and cross my arms over my chest. The guys are just a few feet ahead, playing on the water-kissed sand.

Noah turns and runs toward me, his eye on the frisbee. I stop in my tracks because he isn't looking where he's going. He jumps with his arm stretched out and catches the plastic disc. His feet land on uneven sand.

"Oh, fuck," he says, stumbling and almost face planting into a bystander's cooler. "Sorry man." He holds his hand up to the stranger as an apology.

"You good?" I ask.

Noah looks at me wide eyed, as if he'd forgotten I was here. A toothy grin lifts his lips. He tosses the frisbee to Ethan then traps my face between his hands and pulls me in for a kiss. Heat climbs my neck to my cheeks again. If I wasn't on the verge of a sunburn, there'd be no hiding it.

Noah pulls back when Ethan starts yelling about their game. He presses his forehead to mine and says, "I am now."

Damn this man.

Damn these butterflies that I can't control and the painful ache of want rippling through me.

Damn him for being a good—no great—fake boyfriend.

And damn me for wanting this to be real.

Noah grabs my hand and we walk back to the guys. My mind is spinning, caught in a vortex of the past and present. I'm struggling to keep the two separate because this is a page ripped out of my past that the love-gods have copy and pasted, almost to the tee.

The boys don't jump back into their game. They talk about their plans for tonight. I half-half listen, too focused on the way Noah's thumb is rubbing circles on my skin. Out of nowhere, I remember why I came down here and blurt, "Gemma's ready to go. Preston is falling asleep."

"Thanks!" Ethan tosses the frisbee to Rob and jogs past us up to his umbrella. No one complains as he leaves, or calls him pussy whipped, like they would have before the baby. The guys just let him go and continue their conversation.

Apparently the boys are having a bachelor party tonight while us girls go out. Not the smartest idea in my opinion, but not my wedding either. I listen to them talk about the bars they want to go to.

"Think there are any strip clubs around here?" Rob asks.

I snort, unsurprised that he wants to see titties. Rob's eyes dart toward me and Noah pulls me closer. He tucks me under his arm, protectively, and I don't even care that he's sweaty.

"Hey, babe?" I look up at Noah. If he's surprised to hear me use a pet name he hides it well. My heart races. Asking for his room key shouldn't be this nerve racking but we haven't discussed sleeping arrangements. I assumed he'd be in his room and I'd be in mine and no one would be the wiser. "Can I get the room key? I'm ready to go in."

There's a glimmer of disaster in his eyes. I feel the crack of doubt grow wider, panic overriding my senses. He won't say no in front of Rob, but what happens when we're out of earshot. Will he say I've gone too far?

Noah bends and grabs my thighs. He lifts me over his shoulder, then smacks my ass. "We're out," is all he says to the guys. That should have been it. An easy exit, but where my ex is involved, nothing is easy.

"Get a room," Rob mumbles.

I flick him off and Rob adds, "A different room. I don't want to hear you two through those paper thin walls."

Noah stops, and spins. I can't see the guys anymore as he walks backward up the sand, but I can hear them (obviously), though I wish I couldn't.

"You know how Harper gets when you find that magic button. Even with a pillow over her face the neighbors can hear," Noah taunts. "Or maybe you don't?"

"Fuck you, Noah. I've made Harper come more times than you can count."

"How many times did you scream my name last night, Starlight? Five?"

"Six," I add, already regretting answering.

Rob was amazing in bed during the beginning of our relationship. But, like everything else, he stopped trying. I faked it more often than not because lord knows his ego couldn't take the blow. Now though, I hope he's second guessing every time I screamed his name because it was only ever once per bedroom romp.

I've already dived down this rabbit hole, might as well keep digging. "I about died from embarrassment when I had to call the front desk for new sheets. I don't know how you made me squirt like that at the end, but you've gotta do it again."

Rob makes a disgusted face and jogs past us to the umbrella. He practically tackles Lydia and pushes her onto the sand. He cups her breast in one hand while mauling her mouth with his tongue. It's disgusting. So much so that Ethan's parents decide to leave.

Noah carries me all the way to the boardwalk then sets me on my feet. "That was great. I'm proud of you."

"It was fun watching him squirm," I admit. "Oh, crap. I forgot to grab our shoes."

"Hang on. I'll go get them." Noah jogs back down to our umbrella. He finds our shoes, his shirt, and my coverup—all of which have been thoroughly covered in sand thanks to Rob's newest attempt at PG-13 beach porn —and shakes them out. He jogs back up to the boardwalk and we walk in silence to the lobby.

When we reach the elevator he looks around, then says, "Do you want to stop on the third floor and grab your things?"

"What? Why would I do that?" The doors slide open and we step inside. I lean against the metal bar and press my back against the mirrored wall. It's cold, but feels amazing against my hot skin.

"I'm lost. I thought you were coming to my room?"

"Fuck, Noah. I'm sorry. I keep dragging you into my shit. Gemma asked me what room I was in in front of Lydia and I couldn't tell her the truth. She thinks we're dating and I panicked." I close my eyes and drop my head back against the glass. "I feel like I'm ruining your wedding-get-away."

"I promise, there's no one I'd rather have as my fake-date than you." He hip bumps me and I bite back a grin. "Bring your stuff up. Rob's room is next to mine. At the very least, he's going to expect to see you in there for the next hour. Might as well get ready for this evening."

"Hour?"

"You didn't honestly think we'd be a fifteen minute fuck. Did you?" Noah's lips lift in the corner and I laugh.

If I could get out of my head, pretending to be with him would be easy. We mesh in a way I haven't with anyone else. But there's the lingering thought of what happens when this is over? Will I be able to push him to the back burner like I did this year, and move on with my life? Will he become a staple like he used to be before everything turned upside down?

Or will I be kicking myself because I've opened Pandora's box?

The elevator doors open again on my floor. Noah walks with me to my room and waits as I repack my life. It takes less than five minutes for me to gather my things. I have one suitcase, unzipped on the bed waiting to be dealt with. My clothes from earlier are on the bathroom floor, and my toiletry bag is on the counter. I stuff the loose items in my suitcase and do one last walk through to make sure I haven't forgotten anything.

Noah grabs the handle of my bag before the zipper rounds its track. He rolls it behind him as we make our way up to his room. This time, we listen to the music as we ride to his floor. Some pop song I recognize but don't know plays in the background. Noah hums to it and I'm taken back to yet another memory I'd thought was forgotten.

It's mentally and emotionally exhausting being ripped out of the present and into the past. We have a few hours before tonight's get-together. After a hot shower, I might just take a nap.

Noah's suite is twice the size of my old room, with a separate living room, a pull out couch, mini kitchen, and balcony overlooking the pool. The king size bed doesn't swallow the floor like the full bed did in my room. There's room to breathe which makes me feel better about encroaching on his space. I walk to the sliding glass door and tug it open and look out at the ocean.

"I'm going to run down to the front desk for a few." Noah drags my bag into the bedroom, then meets me on the balcony. He leans onto the railing, the muscles of his arms flexing beneath his weight. "I want to know if you check out today if they can comp you the other nights."

"Why would I check out?"

"Because I've already decided you're staying with me."

"Noah…"

He covers my mouth with his hand. "Shut up. I refuse to hear your excuses. My room is plenty big. I'll take the pull out couch if you're too chicken shit to sleep next to me, but you're staying. End of story."

I nod and he sets my mouth free. I turn away from the sun and lean my ass against the railing. "I doubt they will give me any money back."

"You never know. I have a way with words."

"Meaning you'll make up some extravagant lie?"

He shrugs, which means yes. "Why don't you take a shower while I'm gone and get ready? Your girls' night will be here before you know it."

I groan. "Don't remind me."

"Relax." He reaches for my hand. "You'll be fine."

Chapter 7

HARPER

THE WARM WATER beats down on me, releasing the tension in my shoulders. I tilt my head, letting the beads drip from one side of my neck to the other. When the bathroom is more steam than air, and I'm a little more relaxed, I shut the shower head off.

I wrap a towel around me, tuck a corner in between my boobs, then press my hand to the mirror and wipe a space clean to get a look at myself. What's left of my eyeliner is smudged and my hair that was up in a messy just-been-fucked looking bun needs a quick blow before straightening, but overall I don't look as exhausted as I feel.

After wiping away what's left of my makeup, I step out into the main sleeping area, expecting to be alone, but there's Noah, lying on the bed, scaring the living shit out of me because for a hot second I forgot I was in *his* bathroom. My towel slips as I start and I scream.

Noah's eyes trail over my very naked (but thankfully now shaven) body. "Damn, Starlight. That's how you make an entrance."

"What the hell are you doing, Noah?" I bend down, scrambling for the towel, then wrap myself up again.

"I was watching TV, but got a little distracted." He winks and it's the most playboy thing I think I've ever seen him do. The line is so cringy, the facial tick so uncharacteristically spastic, I can't help but laugh.

"You need to work on your pickups." I sit on the edge of the bed, one leg underneath me. The mattress is big enough Noah doesn't have to scoot. He lays directly in the center and I still have space to roam. "What happened at the concierge desk?"

"I told the woman I proposed to you and that you said yes, so we'd like to check out of your room. She made me give her all the details—if anyone asks I set out two dozen candles on the beach and wrote will you marry me in roses. You cried—and the woman at the desk refunded the whole weekend. She even gave us breakfast." He holds up two vouchers, then tosses them aside. "Do anything dirty while I was gone?"

That's a relief. I'm sure it'll take a few days for the money to hit the bank, but now I won't have to choose between dinner this weekend and gas. I shove his shoulder, in a glorious mood and say, "You wish."

Noah scoots closer and shifts onto one side. He leans in and whispers, "Hey, Harper?"

"Yeah?"

"You're naked in my bed."

I am. Aren't I? In a moment of stupidity, or maybe bravery, I decide to say what I want, even though we're alone and there's no reason for us to pretend. But if there's even the slightest chance I haven't been reading too deeply into today and there's some brewing between us again, I've got to know. "What are you gonna do about it?"

Noah wraps his fingers around the back of my neck and pulls me into him. His lips don't ask permission. They take what they want without apology. He devours me, our kiss a heady mixture of teeth and moans and gasps. I touch his hair, neck, arms. He tugs at my towel, exposing all of me.

He pulls back and takes me in. I'm not ashamed of my body or the way he's looking at me. I think Noah likes what he sees. His mouth drops to my nipple and he sucks it in, flicking the ball of my ring with his tongue. Teasing. Taunting.

The vague memory of him threatening my pussy with a good time comes to mind and I believe him when he said his tongue was almost as good as his dick because *wow!*

Noah pushes me onto my back and his hand runs down my side. It caresses my hip, then dives between my legs. I spread for him, expecting to feel his fingers inside me but am met with a new sensation.

Noah slides down and kisses my folds. He licks, and laps, and nips until my back arches and then, only then, does he stick his fingers inside.

I claw at his head, with the intention of grabbing hair, but making my body do anything besides come seems impossible. The pressure builds inside me and I feel it, an explosion of all explosions. I dig my fingers into the mattress. My legs close on instinct and try to scoot away but Noah holds them open. He makes me enjoy the ride and, fuck me, it's good. He senses I'm at the end because he switches his finger for his tongue and my liquid heat covers his mouth while I pant his name. When I'm done, he sits up and wipes me from his mouth with the back of his hand.

"What the hell was that?" I ask, breathless and coming down from a high better than any drug could give.

Noah smirks before he makes me taste my sweet musk on his lips. It's intoxicating.

I want more.

I reach for his belt. He promised his dick was better than that and while I'm not sure I believe it's possible to reach a greater level of pleasure, I'm ready to find out. I don't get the chance.

Noah grips my wrist, stopping my hand from dipping beneath his waistline. He holds my gaze and whispers, "No."

"Why not?" I'm not begging, but damn if that's what he wants to hear I will. I'll drop down to my knees and literally beg Noah to let me suck him off, because let's be real. What will start as a blow job will end with his dick inside me. No one actually likes giving head.

"Fuck," Noah grumbles. He runs his fingers through his hair and rolls onto his back.

I grab my towel and wrap it around myself. Seconds tick by where he doesn't move or say anything. The longer we sit the more it sinks in that he regrets what we've just done and I feel like shit.

Useless.

A little used.

"Harper...I..."

"It's fine, Noah." I cut him off. Tears sting my eyes but I refuse to let them fall. Not now when the hurt is so fresh and he can see the pain. "I think I want to take a nap. It's probably going to be a late night. Is that okay?"

"Yeah." Noah stands and fixes his clothes. "I've...uh...got some shit to do anyway." He digs a key out of his wallet and drops it on the bedside table. "Text me if you need anything. Okay?"

"Sure thing." I force a smile then walk to the bathroom and shut the door. I slide down it, not bothering to fight the tears rolling down my cheeks.

I bite my lip to stay quiet but once the room door shuts, I let it all out.

Chapter 8

NOAH

I SLAM my hand against the wall next to the elevator . It doesn't make me feel any better. If I could, I would use my fist, but I don't want to get kicked out of the hotel for destruction of property. That would ruin Ethan and Gemma's wedding and leave Harper alone, both of which I refuse to do.

I run my fingers through my hair and pull at the roots, unsure of what to do next. I'm fucked. So deeply, immeasurably, fucked.

I can still taste Harper's juices on my tongue. It's devine hell. The forbidden fruit I shouldn't have eaten because

I want more.

I can't go back to being *just friends*. Before, when I'd forgotten what it felt like to be her world, I was surviving at best. Having her as a friend was better than not having her at all. After what just went down, that's what's going to happen. I'm going to lose Harper for good.

I never should have taken advantage of her when her guard was down.

I. Am. An asshole.

I kick the trash can. Its metal lid goes flying across the hallway.

More noise.

More reasons for people to call security.

Ethan is the only one to open his door and pokes his head out. The whole wedding party is on this floor, minus Harper's original room, as well as a few random guests. Most of our crew is still at the beach, but there's a chance someone we don't know could be in their room calling security because there's a lunatic outside their door throwing a fit.

"You good?" Ethan asks.

"Fine," I say through gritted teeth.

He eyes me, brows bunching together and I know I've fucked up. He closes the door, disappearing inside for a minute. I push the elevator button two, three, four times, with every intent to ghost his ass. I don't want to explain what's going on, but Ethan steps out of his room and is by my side before it can *ding.*

The doors slide open a few seconds later and we wordlessly get inside. He presses the L-button. We ride down to the lobby. I wait for him to ask what my malfunction is, already coming up with excuses in my head.

Harper and I got into a fight. Nope can't say that. He'll press me for details and I don't want to lie.

Rob is a dick and won't leave my girlfriend alone. The only truth in that statement is that her ex is a dick.

I'm a fucking idiot in love with my best friend even though she's acted like I didn't exist this past year; and oh yeah, I just ate her out. How was it you ask? Great! I had her shaking and begging for more. But then ran out like a chicken shit pussy.

"I need a drink," Ethan says once we're on the ground floor.

I nod, because honestly I could use one myself. I thought having a clear mind was what I needed to remain in control but clearly that was a failed plan.

I grit my teeth and head to the bar. It's packed but we get an order in.

Ethan and I take our bucket of beers to the boardwalk. We both lean on the railing and look out at the ocean. The tide has come in, stealing about twelve feet of the shoreline, but the people sitting out by the water don't seem to mind.

"I don't think I've ever seen you this happy," Ethan muses. He twists the cap off his beer and tosses it into the ice cold bucket. I take a bottle and do the same. "Sucks shit between you two is fake."

I choke on my drink. I didn't hear him right. Our charade is flawless to the point I almost believe our bull shit. "Excuse me?"

"Come on, man. You've had a thing for that girl since before we met. You expect me to believe y'all got together and you kept that shit to yourself?"

I don't have a response.

What's there to say? Ethan is right.

If this thing between Harper and I were real, I would have called him up the day I convinced her to give me a chance and spilled the beans. Instead I expected him to live a one liner just because we've kissed in public. *Fuck*. "Rob made Harper feel uncomfortable. On a whim, she told him we were dating and I ran with it."

"This is the chance you've been waiting for, brother." Ethan notices my beer is empty. He hands me another even though he bought the bucket and his drink has barely been touched. "So, why were you acting like a little bitch in the hallway? What went wrong?"

"Nothing."

Everything.

I sigh, exhausted from the emotional whiplash of this. Maybe letting everything out would be good. Ethan already knows the truth. What harm could come from getting some outside perspective. "I took advantage of her."

"No, you didn't," he replies before I can finish the sentence. There's no faux sympathy or coddling in his tone. It's hard and direct, like he believes every word of what he says.

But he's wrong.

"Yes, I did. Harper is emotionally vulnerable and I went and stuck my tongue in her. Literally."

He laughs and takes another swallow of his drink. "At least it wasn't your dick."

"It could have been! She wanted me to fuck her and I told her no. I left her on the bed, naked, like a total dick." I run my fingers through my hair because if I don't do something with my hands I'm going to end up punching something, maybe even someone.

"Damn, dude." Ethan chuckles and I can't possibly imagine how this situation is funny.

Not only did I take advantage of Harper, she probably thinks I used her too. I should just tattoo *asshole* on my forehead so she and every other girl will stay the fuck away.

I finish my second beer and take the third, the last one in the bucket. I might as well enjoy myself because I'm staying as far from Harper as possible. I'll sleep on the beach or on one of the pool hammocks tonight if I have to. I doubt that woman will want to look, let alone sleep under the same roof as me after what I've done.

Ethan claps his hand on my shoulder and gives me *the look*. It almost makes me laugh thinking about how his son is going to get the same look from him thirteen years from now—give or take—but then I remember I'm the asshole needing to be talked to like a fucking teenager because I can't keep my dick in my pants.

"Sounds like you have two options. One, be the best damn fake boyfriend Harper has ever had. Woo her. Make her wish things between you two were real. Dick her down so good she'll be touching herself to the memory for weeks. Then tell her the truth, that you want this." He pauses to let the weight of it all sink in. But he's not done. "Or, avoid her tonight, do the bare minimum tomorrow, and part ways as soon as the reception is over. You can go back to the pathetic relationship you called friendship and everything will stay the way it's been for the past ten years. Your call, bro."

I pick at the paper label on my bottle. I've drunk half of the contents already and wish for once in my life I was a lightweight. It would be nice to forget this shit and roll with the punches, but Ethan is right.

I have a decision to make and no matter which I choose, everything between Harper and me is gonna change.

Chapter 9

HARPER

I SEE Noah for all of two minutes before filing into the limousine Gemma's mom got us for the night. He doesn't come over to say hi or hug me. He doesn't smile in my direction or give even an iota of recognition that I'm in the same room. He purposefully stands with his back to us girls, so there's no chance we'll have to look at each other.

It's the final knife in my gut.

I'm ripped open, bleeding embarrassment and shame for all the world to see and yet no one notices. The girls—Gemma, Lydia, and six others whose names I've heard but don't remember—pop open a bottle of champagne and eat up my fake smiles like they're chocolate.

One of the girls, a pretty red-head, hands out glasses. I take mine and stare at the bubbles. There's no denying I have an addictive personality. I ruined myself with drinking, drugs, and letting Rob use me up. I know this, just like I know that I will always struggle. A little voice will whisper in my mind to give in to my old vices every time the world gets hard and it's my job to say no.

Today that voice isn't whispering, it's yelling. Screaming that I'll feel better if I just take a sip.

I want to.

I want to numb the pain of being around Gemma and pretending I'm fine. I want to silence the voices that tell me I'm not good enough for Noah and that these fake moments will be all I'll ever have. I want to erase the memories I've made with both my exes and live in the comfortable numb spaces again.

"Here's to your last night of freedom!" one of the girls calls out. The others cheer and raise their glasses. I do the same, another smile in place no one notices is fake.

We clink our classes together. Everyone drinks half the liquid in their flute right off the bat. I bring mine to my lips and pretend, but don't swallow. Something else no one notices. It never seems to shock me how lonely life can be, even when surrounded by people.

"I haven't had a night of freedom since Preston was born." Gemma laughs, finishing her drink, and one of the girls refills her flute.

I connect my phone to the bluetooth speaker and pull up an old playlist. "Wannabe" by the Spice Girls is the first up and everyone starts singing into their glasses. I grab Gemma's phone and open the camera app to record because this is one of those epic Tik Tok moments that will probably go viral.

Gemma downs her glass like we've jumped back into our college days and, thanks to her friends, it's refilled almost as soon as it's empty. Three more drinks and she'll be on the path to getting drunk. No judgment. She deserves to let loose.

———

The night has passed in a blur of bar hopping, late night food truck stops, and dancing. It doesn't feel close to winding down. We've found our way to a country bar near the beach that has karaoke on the outside patio and a band inside. Our table is semi-close to the stage and I have officially dubbed myself the purse watcher.

"Drink." Lydia sets a yellow shot on the high top table in front of me.

"Thanks." I hold the glass in my hand and smile. I've forced so many tonight, my cheeks hurt.

"Naw, bitch. I want to see you take it." Lydia arches her eyebrows at me and waits. "You've been a sourpuss all night and it's killing the vibe. Drink. Let go. And have some fun. For all we fucking know, you're gonna ghost our asses for two more years and I'll have to clean up the mess you leave."

"What are you talking about?"

"Gemma!" Lydia throws her hands in the air. "Good lord, you're an idiot. That woman misses you. That woman has done nothing but talk about how excited she is to see your ass. You finally show up for a night out and you choose to sit by yourself. So." She takes my shot and lifts it closer to my face. "Fuckin' drink, bitch."

She's right.

I've been a Debby-downer all night and when I thought no one noticed, she did. Maybe Lydia isn't so bad after all. She just has shit taste in men.

Then again, Rob is my ex. So what does that say about me?

I take the shot from her and stare at it. It's been a long time since I've touched a drop of alcohol. I'm nervous. I don't want to be puking tomorrow, but if I stop at just one I should be fine. This, after all, is a celebration.

I suck in a breath and close my eyes. *I can do this.*

The drink is snatched from my fingers before the first drop can reach my lips. I snap my eyes open, equal parts pissed and relieved. Noah tosses my shot back then slams the glass on the table. "Whoo!" he yells. "That shit was sour. Lemon drop?"

"Noah!" Lydia squeals. She shoves his shoulder playfully. "That was Harper's!"

"Really? Couldn't tell." He winks and drapes his arm over my shoulder. Where we've all dressed up for the night, Noah is still in his bathing suit and a shirt. The other guys aren't much fancier, in shorts and flip flops.

"What are you doing here?" I ask, genuinely curious. I was under the impression that tonight we were doing our own things and not seeing each other until the wedding tomorrow afternoon.

"Ethan got a drunk text from Gemma. Most of it was gibberish but she said something about butt-sex so he came running." Noah laughs and nuzzles into my neck. "I missed you, Starlight." His breath smells like lemons and beer, but I love the way it lingers on my skin. His tongue tease my neck, brushing against me with a featherlight touch.

"You're drunk." My heart hammers in my chest. I turn toward him. Our lips are a whisper away. I could easily close the space between us, but I want him to make the choice.

I want him to choose me.

"And you're beautiful." He does, if only for the sake of our audience. Noah leans forward and kisses me. One, painfully simple kiss that makes me want more than he's willing to give. "I have a surprise for you. Outside."

"I don't know. We shouldn't leave Gemma…"

Noah covers my mouth with his hand. "If I wanted your lips, Starlight, they'd be around my dick." He waits for the shock to pass, then cups my cheeks. "But I want you, Harper Herron. All of you."

Our foreheads touch and for a split second I forget that all of this is fake. I close my eyes and chose not to think about tomorrow, or even five seconds from now. I fall into this moment and how being with Noah feels like home.

"Now move that fine ass." He pulls back and smacks my butt. The sequined dress I've got on rides up my thighs. Noah's fingers graze the skin beneath my cheeks. It's hard to tell in the dim lighting, but I think he blushes when he says, "And get outside."

Chapter 10

HARPER

I'M GOING to kill him.

Straight up murder this man.

My *surprise* is the equivalent of stepping into hell. I followed a beautiful devil into the deep and wish I would have stayed back inside where I was safe. I was happy sipping my soda and people watching. Drunks make the best entertainment. I should know. I used to be one.

The DJ at the front of the patio hands Noah a microphone and holds another out for me. There's a makeshift stage, with colorful lights, two mic-stands, and speakers on either side. Noah hops onto the center of it and the color drains from my face. I haven't been on stage since the eighth grade talent show where we pulled an epic but one-time Backstreet Boys performance.

I looked over at Gemma, who has followed us outside as well as the rest of the group. Everyone is here: the bride and groom, Rob, Lydia, and everyone else who's name I can't remember. Ethan wraps his arms around Gemma's waist. She leans against him and watches us. Waiting for the show I have zero intentions of being a part of to start.

They all do.

The music starts and a tiny, *tiny* bit of my nervousness lifts. The beginning chords of "I Want It That Way" by the epic boy band plays through the speakers. The words are projected on a small computer screen in the corner of the DJ stage but I don't need the lyrics. Every word is tattooed on my heart. I could sing this song with my eyes closed.

I just hope we're only singing.

"You are, my fire. The one, desire." Noah takes the first verse. He reaches for my hand and pulls me into his chest. I look into his eyes, feeling like a schoolgirl again. My heart races, stupidly falling for the act.

He trails his finger across my cheek, laying his drool worthy pop star act on thick. I duck my head, remembering how we used to do this as kids. In middle school, I was obsessed with the Backstreet Boys and Noah loved to feed my obsession by pretending to be one. That's how far back things between us go, to the days before I realized what this ache in my chest meant.

Noah's knuckle settles under my chin. He lifts my face and looks at me like I'm the only girl in the world. I want so badly to believe it, but the nagging thought that our feelings aren't the same won't leave me alone.

His act is wasted on me, the girl who will forever be stuck in the friend zone. I'd bet a dollar that every woman at the bar knows this song. Any one of those beautiful ladies could be up here, in my place, letting him serenade them. The difference is with them he'd get laid, where as with me...he made it clear this afternoon that sex will never happen.

"Believe, when I say, I want it that way." Noah backs up a step, crosses his legs, and spins once, in full boy band mode. He crosses the stage down to where Gemma is and pulls her out of Ethan's arms. He twirls her around then hands her back to her future husband.

I panic because this is how it started, our choreography—instead of dancing with Gemma, it was me in his arms. I'm expected to sing the next verse, and dance, and be happy when all I want to do is crawl into a dark corner and hide.

Noah spreads his fingers, covering his heart then turns and then side steps up to the stage again. The chorus sings, giving him a chance to shine before stepping in with his invisible boy band.

The chorus ends which means it's almost my turn. I take a deep breath, pushing back my nerves, and lift the microphone. Noah's eyes light up. I think he hoped I'd reprise my role, but didn't expect it. As much as I don't want to, he's had my back today. It would be fucked up if I didn't support him, even if he's asking me to sing this amazing but stupid song.

"Am I, your fire?" My voice is shaky but not completely off key, which is a relief. Middle school me took this verse and made it like I was asking the world did it want me. Tonight I'm changing it up. I don't look at the crowd. I stare at Noah and sing only to him. I touch his chest and push him onto the railing that separates us from the sidewalk. His legs spread and I step between them, getting as close as I can with the microphone between us "Your one desire?"

I pretend the world isn't watching. I run my fingers through his hair. I'm in complete control of this moment, but my verse is ending. I step back and find the mic-stand. I can't get my mic in the holder. I'm struggling, making extra noise as I sing "...but I want it that way."

Noah grabs my arm and pulls me to him. "Tell me why?"

I look up into his eyes and sing the next line, even though our invisible boy band sings it for us. We go back and forth, pretending to ask each other the questions of the song and answering them. We should be dancing, pointing at each other and box-stepping around the stage. But Noah's hand slides from my arm to my lower back. There isn't enough room for both microphones between us. I lower mine and sing into his.

The melody changes, and I realize the serious part of the song is almost over. This is the part where Noah is supposed to drop to his knees, basically cursing the world for his love pains. It's a sight to see when the whole routine is done. He doesn't look like he's going to sing the line.

I turn in his arms and raise my mic. "Don't wanna hear you saaaay!"

Noah doesn't let me go. He holds my body tight to his and rocks our hips. I grind against him and try to finish the song. When the last line is sung, Noah whispers it in my ear so low the microphone almost doesn't pick it up.

I look over my shoulder.

Noah is a good man. Far better than any I deserve. He takes my microphone and hands it back to the DJ. The next couple comes up to the stage. I don't listen to what they sing. I don't care. All I can think about is Noah's hand on my lower back. It's loud outside, so he leans close to ask, "You want a drink?"

I nod and far too soon he's gone.

"That was adorable!" Lydia shouts. "How long were you planning that routine?"

Fifteen years, give or take some improvised moments. "Not long, but Noah and I have history with that song."

"And every pop song from the early two-thousands," Rob grumbles. Lydia nudges him with her elbow, but Rob doesn't take the hint. He never does. "Any time a song came on she knew it was always met with *Noah and I did this* or *Noah and I used to do that.* Fucking drove me crazy."

"No one asked you to be here, Rob." I cross my arms over my chest. "You could leave anytime."

"Like you?" He pulls a joint from his cigarette case and lights it. The smell coils around my senses. I want a hit but will never take a thing from that man again. He exhales and blows the smoke in my face. "Who asked you to come back?"

"Gemma." I got the invitation via Facebook. She didn't have my address, so it couldn't be mailed. When I called her to say I was coming, she was thrilled.

"Did she though?"

"Rob. Enough," Lydia urges, but the prick ignores her.

He keeps digging, searching for that tender spot in me that will cause the most damage. He finds it. "Did she call you to tell you she was engaged? Did she tell you about the bridal shower last month? Or invite you out to Vegas for the bachelorette party?" He laughs, realizing that his assumptions are true and takes another hit from his joint. "Didn't think so. You're here because they pity you. No one wants you here, Harper. Not even Noah."

"Leave Noah out of this." I feel like I'm going to puke. He's wrong. I know he is. Gemma is my friend. She wanted me here to celebrate with them.

"But he's the icing on the cake, sweetheart." Rob blows another cloud at me and grins. "He didn't tell anyone you were dating until *you* outed his dirty little secret."

It's not true. I know this, but for some reason the altered truth stings.

"Harper," Lydia starts but her sentence trails off. It's all the confirmation I need.

Gemma never wanted me here. We didn't talk every day, my schedule at the diner and hers with Preston made that hard, but we did our best. Now that I think about it, she never brought up the wedding. Not once, unless I asked. I didn't think it was odd at the time, but now I do.

"Excuse me," I say, leaving without offering anyone a goodbye. The more I think about it, the harder Rob's words hit. Even tonight, while I sulked at a table she left me alone. Lydia was the only person to pay me any attention all night. I thought it might be her trying to forge a friendship. I understand now, it was pity.

Chapter 11

HARPER

I WIPE my tears as they stream down my cheeks.

I feel stupid. I should have listened to my gut and left before this whole weekend started. I would still be in the bubble where my best friend liked me and there was no confusion when it came to Noah. He was to be kept an arm's length away.

Period.

I had figured out how to self soothe and not ache to feel his touch. I learned to exist in a world without him and now all I want is to find Noah and cry into his arms, but I won't ruin his night. I've robbed too many from him over the years as it is.

"Harper!" Noah calls.

I wipe my face again and turn toward the sound of his voice. I hug myself to keep from reaching for him. He would embrace me without question, but I feel the cycle starting over. I can't begin to count the nights Rob made me cry and Noah was there for every one of them. Talking me off a ledge. Making me feel like someone worth being with.

"Where are you going?" he asks.

"Go back to the party, Noah," I say, turning away. I need to get to the hotel and grab my things. There's no reason for me to stay, not when I wasn't wanted. If I start driving now, I can make it to the Georgia state line and to one of my diners before the breakfast shift starts. Martha, my boss, can always use an extra hand. I'm sure she wouldn't mind working me onto the schedule.

"Hey." He grabs my arm and pulls me close. "Have you been crying?"

I try to look away but he takes my chin between his fingers. My lip wobbles. I bite my cheek to keep the tears at bay, but one slips loose. Noah pushes it away with his thumb and frowns down at me.

"I'm fine," I insist, but he's not buying it.

"Damn it, woman," he mumbles. His arms wrap tight around me as he pulls me into his chest. As much as I want to fight this feeling, being held like this is what I needed. "What happened?"

"Rob happened."

"That fucker. I swear, he's going to end up with a broken nose before the weekend is over. What did he do?"

"Nothing."

"Harper," he says in a warning tone.

Noah arches back to look down at me. I can't meet his gaze, but I can't stay in his arms either. I step back and sigh. This fantasy I've created with Noah didn't even last twenty-four hours, but its short run was nice. I need to leave before the pain of saying goodbye sets in, but I owe him an explanation of why. "He didn't do anything but tell me the truth."

"What are you talking about?"

"This!" I throw my arms up in the air. "No one wants me here, Noah. Gemma invited me on Facebook. I didn't get invited to her actual bachelorette party. Tonight's *one last hoorah* was bullshit. I'm not going to be where I'm not wanted. I'm going home."

"I want you."

"No, you don't, Noah. You can't."

"You don't know what I want," he insists, but he's wrong. I do. I know everything there is to know about Noah, just like he knows me. We can lie to ourselves, but not each other.

"You want me to feel safe, and I love you for that." I take his hands and squeeze. This is it. The moment where we say goodbye. It hits me that I probably won't come back to Florida again. I have no family. My parents died in a car accident three years ago and I'm an only child, as were they. Noah is my only tie to this state, and I can't go back to being just friends. Not now that I know what I'd be missing. "But you should be enjoying yourself, fucking a pretty girl you'll never see again or whatever it is guys do at bachelor parties, not worrying about me."

Noah's eyebrows furrow. He cups my cheeks and looks down at me. "The only girl I want to fuck tonight is you, Harper."

I stare at him, wide eyed. Completely shocked.

"I always want to fuck you. You've been in my head since the moment I first slid my dick inside that perfect pussy of yours when we were fifteen, so if it happens again it won't be a one time thing. I want you for as long as you'll have me. Forever if I have my way."

I can't find words. Or thoughts. My mind is stuck on the fact that Noah wants me. He's always wanted me.

"But I can't risk being with you if you're going to walk away. Stay for me, Harper." He presses his forehead to mine and whispers, "Stay."

"Okay." I'm crying again, only this time I'm not sad. I'm happy, so unbelievably happy.

Noah's mouth slants on mine. His tongue presses between my lips, not waiting for an invitation. I tangle my fingers in his hair. He grips my thighs and lifts me into the air. My legs wrap around his waist and our bodies mold into each other.

Noah carries me to the dunes and lays me on the sand. He kisses my cheek. Jaw. Neck. Devouring me with his mouth as his hand slips up the skirt of my dress. The sand is cold, but my skin is on fire.

Noah tugs my panties aside with his finger and teases my entrance. I shudder in anticipation, wanting nothing more than to feel him inside of me.

Voices carrying from the sidewalk twenty feet away give me reason to pause but Noah doesn't notice. He pushes his index finger deep inside me, then moves it in and out. I hold my breath, terrified to make a sound, but unable to keep my pleasure a secret.

I pant his name. Noah takes my wrist and lowers it to his cock. I slip beneath the elastic band of his board shorts and boxers and grip his thick, smooth shaft. I rub my thumb over the precum at its tip and he sticks another finger inside me. The pleasure is intense. I can't get enough.

"Noah," I gasp. My thoughts are coming in broken pieces. Pressure swells in my center. I'm close. So beautifully close to coming. "Someone might see us."

Noah's warm breath fans my neck. "Let them watch, Starlight. The world needs to know you're mine."

I. Am. His.

That's all I need to hear. I tug Noah's cock free and line him up with my center. He presses against the opening, teasing me with pressure, but doesn't go inside.

"We need a condom."

I rock my hips, aching to feel him. "I'm on the pill."

It's what he needs to hear. Noah thrusts his hips, sinking deep inside me. I cry out in a heady mix of pain and pleasure. My walls throb around him as they adjust to his thickness. He fills me to the point that I don't know how we're going to have sex. The thought of him going deeper is terrifying but I want him.

Noah peppers my nose, lips, cheeks with kisses. "You okay, beautiful?"

I nod.

He starts slow, sliding in and out of me with tortuous pleasure. My knees bend and I instinctively want to retreat. The sensation is too great, too perfect. He grabs my thighs and sets one leg on each shoulder, picking up pace. I writhe beneath him, beautifully close to an orgasm. Noah's hand goes to my neck and his thick fingers wrap around it. The gentle pressure sends me over the edge.

I cry out, "Noah," as liquid heat coats him. He silences me with a dirty kiss and somehow pushes deeper inside me. My body trembles with delight, another release chasing the first.

Noah pulls out, but he doesn't come. "On your knees, beautiful."

I flip over and stick my ass in the air. Noah spits on his dick and enters me again. He pumps twice then pulls me upright by my hair. I love the pain because behind it is pleasure.

I'm panting hard, unable to believe I'm having sex with Noah. Never in my wildest dreams did I picture this, but it's better than anything I could have imagined.

Noah pushes me back onto my elbows. His fingers dig into my hips and I can feel a change in his pace. It's faster, deeper. I reach between my legs and grab his balls. I don't remember who taught me the move, but it's something I've learned enhances the male orgasm. Noah had made me feel so good tonight, I want to do the same.

His stride fumbles and he moans. "Dear god, woman." He jerks a few more times then empties inside of me.

Noah tugs his shirt off and pulls out. I sit on the fabric and let his seed drip out. We stare at the ocean and listen to the waves roll onto shore. The silence isn't uncomfortable, but it's not great either.

"Now what?" I ask.

Sitting on the beach with ripped underwear (don't know when or how that happened) and on a come covered shirt, I feel vulnerable. In my experience, men talk a big game to get into your pants but once they're there, everything after is a let down.

I don't want to think Noah is like the rest, but I can't help but to expect to be hurt.

"Skinny dipping." He looks over at me and grins. That smile, the same one I fell in love with in the seventh grade that broke my heart the year I turned sixteen, the smile that could turn every bad day around, sends a burst of liquid heat through my veins again.

"Is that so?"

"Yup." Noah leans over and claims my mouth again. A sandy hand cups the back of my head, holding us close even after the kiss breaks. "We're gonna get you clean so I can dirty you again. We've got ten years to make up for, Starlight. I'm not wasting a single minute."

Chapter 12

HARPER

NOAH and I spent most of the night getting to know each other again. My mouth to his cock. His tongue to my clit. It was an evening of pure bliss with enough come to build a sand castle. At some point, we fell asleep. And now as the sun rises over the horizon, I want nothing more than to crawl under the covers and do it all over again.

Noah brushes the hair away and kisses my forehead. "Morning, Starlight."

"Hey." My voice is raspy. I'm surprised I have one at all considering how many times I cried his name last night. "What time is it?"

Noah finds his phone in the sand and lights up the screen. "Six-thirty. Want to head upstairs for a shower and grab a bite to eat?"

"Yeah. I'm starved."

He helps me slip my dress back on and pulls the zipper for me. I step out of his board shorts and he puts them back on over his boxers. We toss his shirt in the trash because there's enough sperm on it to get a girl pregnant if the wind blows the wrong way. I run my fingers through my hair. They catch every few centimeters on new knots and decide it is unsalvageable. I'm the epitome of the walk of shame—if there ever was one—only I'm proud because my partner is making the walk with me.

We hold hands and trek the three blocks back to the hotel. Once we're inside my bladder reminds me that I haven't peed yet this morning. I'm not looking forward to the after-sex-sting and would rather whimper in private than have Noah worry something might be wrong.

"Why don't you head on up? I'm going to pop into the bathroom for a few and then I'll be there."

"Are you sure?" he asks. "I don't mind waiting."

"I'm good."

Noah nods and I step into the ladies room. The first thing I do is walk to the mirror. I grimace at my reflection. My hair is worse than I thought, matted and sticking up in crazy directions. It paired with my smudged eyeliner and raccoon eyes bring a whole new meaning to the just-been-fucked look. I grab some paper towels and wet them. Black mascara staines the white paper, but after a few minutes of scrubbing I look less early-two-thousands punk rock and more me.

Going pee for the first time since swimming in the ocean is brutal. I bite my knuckle to keep from crying out. I've never been this sore or raw in my life. Now that I've stopped moving, my uterus hurts. I didn't even know that was possible! I would do it again, though. Hell, I'm probably going to have sex with Noah once I go upstairs because the pleasure outweighs the pain.

I wipe, flush, then wash my hands.

For the first time in years, I feel happy. A genuine giddiness I've chased for as long as I can remember fills my veins and it's all because of Noah. If I had known that he was this great, I would have dumped Rob and made my move ages ago.

Forever slinks into my thoughts, but I push it aside. I need to focus on today, and tomorrow. After that, Noah and I can figure out what we are and how to proceed. I'll need a job and a place to live close enough to commute, but not in Palm Beach. I need to be as far away from my past as possible if we're to have a future.

I step out of the bathroom, still high from the thought of what Noah and I could be. They're in a discrete hallway off of the lobby, tucked into a dugout where you can't see someone as soon as they step out the door. The men's room is next to the women's, separated by a few feet, but there are cameras in the corner which keeps the odd location safe.

Rob catches me off guard. He catches me by the throat and pushes me against the wall. His body presses against mine, warm and firm, but wrong. It's invasive, not welcoming like Noah's. I bristle but meet his gaze with a hard stare.

Rob's eyes are bloodshot, his pupils large. He's coming down from the night. I can't begin to guess what he might be on. "Pretty little, Harper."

"What do you want, *Robert?*"

He grunts. He hates his name and we both know it, but he's got me pinned to where fighting would be futile. I need to level the playing field even if I'm only using words.

"I want a second chance. You owe me as much."

I owe him?

For what?

Breaking me into an emotionally battered pseudo-wife? Convincing me I was worthless without him? Teaching me to rely on drugs and alcohol to numb the pain? Or how about making me sleep with his dealer when he was short on cash, because that happened at least once a month. I grit my teeth, too shocked to say anything. The burn of tears wets my eyes and I curse myself for being an emotional cryer. Happy, sad, pissed... it didn't matter. It's my body's go-to reaction, but I refuse to shed a single tear for this man again.

"You ate two thousand dollars worth of gummy bears that night," he says, his voice a low growl. "I got my ass beat and had to repay the debt with interest."

"How was I supposed to know they were laced with fentanyl? You always bought the CBD ones."

"By fucking asking." His hand hits the wall beside me. I flinch and he smirks, thinking he's regaining control again but I will never submit to that man.

"I almost died." The words come out choked.

No one believed me when I said it was an accident. I didn't overdose, but given my track record I could see why I was met with doubt.

The hospital gave me a choice. Rehab or jail. I spent six months in a facility, allowed to have visitors while refusing to see everyone. It was there I realized I had problems that stretched beyond alcoholism.

"Your fucking fault." Rob leans in closer. He brushes his nose against my cheek. I turn my head, wanting no part of what he's offering, while knowing there's a chance his offer might be less than amicable. "But that won't happen again, baby. I'll keep the hard stuff out of the house. It'll be us against the world, just like old times."

"No."

Rob doesn't care that I don't want him, or that his girlfriend is probably a few floors up, waiting in his room. He kisses me, and forces his tongue into my mouth. He tastes like ash and whiskey and something else I can't put a finger on. Something too familiar but lost in my mind. Whatever it is, I don't care to remember. I want him out of my space.

I bite down on his tongue until I draw blood.

Rob rears back. He smacks me across the face and mutters, "Bitch!" He spits blood onto the tile and curses. "You fucking bit me."

"Your fucking fault," I reply, quoting him.

We stare at each other, neither one of us wanting to retreat. He smiles wide, blood staining already yellowed teeth. "How'd she taste?"

"Excuse me?"

"Sorry. I forgot you're a blonde at heart. I'll say it again." Rob leans closer, not touching me this time, but whispering into my ear. "How does she fucking taste, Harper? Lydia. Did she taste like every other girl's pussy I cheated on you with? Or was it sweeter since she was a virgin before I deflowered her?"

It takes me a minute, but then it hits me. That flavor, the *other* I've always associated with him, was the come of someone else. My face pales, and I think I'm going to be sick. Rob laughs, the sound deep and low, and he kisses my cheek.

That's it. The straw that breaks me. I put up with so much, all because I thought he loved me, and the asshole was cheating. Probably starting all the way back to day one.

I shove Rob backward and swing. He catches my wrist before my fist can make contact with his face. He squeezes, determined to make me wince in pain. I bite my cheek, trying my hardest not to give him what he wants but his fingers dig deeper. Eventually it's too much and my reaction is involuntary.

"Now that was, naughty." He tisks. "Do you remember what happens to naughty girls?"

Chapter 13

NOAH

I STEP out of the shower and wrap a towel around my waist. I was hoping Harper would join me. I even left the door cracked so there would be no question about an invitation. Last night was amazing, and even though I'm exhausted, I want to feel her again. She's everything I've wanted and more. Even if the sex was terrible, I'd still want her, but I knew it wouldn't be.

Harper only gets better with age.

"Your turn, beautiful." I hold my towel with one hand and push the bathroom door open the other hand. Depending on how she greets me, I might just let the terry cloth slip and ease us into another sexcapade.

I'm greeted with silence.

"Harper?" I walk to the balcony. She's not there. I cross the room and look out into the hallway.

"Harper!" I shout.

More silence.

I shut the door and grab the first thing out of my suitcase my hands touch. I throw mismatched board shorts and a shirt on, then run out of my room, barefoot.

Something is wrong.

It doesn't take a normal girl this long to go to the bathroom, but especially not Harper. She's the fastest pisser I've met. Even if I account for the elevator stopping on every floor and her getting distracted or striking up a conversation, I sill can't justify the amount of time she's been gone.

I push the elevator button to ride down to the lobby. It buzzes, acknowledging my existence, but doesn't move from the third floor. I bounce on my toes. Nervous energy has me unable to stand still. I push the button again and again until finally the double doors slide open.

The ride is less than a minute to the lobby, but it's too long. I run to the front desk and the same lady who comped Harper's room last night is on duty. "Have you seen a girl with JBF hair and a sparkly dress?"

The girl smirks, thinking she knows what Harper and I were up to last night. She's not wrong, but she's so off base right now it hurts. "Sorry, Mr. Ruckers. I haven't."

"Where are your bathrooms?"

"Down the hall, to your right." She points to an opening I overlooked yesterday. The bathrooms aren't marked and the hallway is offset from this angle, behind a pillar. I would have missed it if she hadn't shown me the way.

I sprint across the lobby, unable to shake the feeling that Harper is in danger.

I round the corner and skid to a stop. My heart crashes to my feet.

Rob's got Harper's hair wrapped around his fist, her cheek pressed against the wall, arms pinned behind her back. From a distance, it looks like she's wearing red lipstick.

She's not.

If watching that prick man-handle my future wife didn't make me want to rip Rob's throat out, knowing he made her bleed does.

Harper sees me coming and grins, but Rob has no clue. He's too busy telling her how he's going to make her his again. I grab Rob's shirt collar and pull him off of her.

Harper's legs give out for the lack of pressure on her body. She falls to the floor and my fist meets Rob's face. Noses bleed more than most parts of the body. They're filled with vessels, and I burst every one Rob has.

He falls to the floor and I step over him. I grip the front of his shirt and hit him again, and again. Jaw. Nose. Eye. I'm not aiming. I just want him to hurt as much as he's hurt Harper.

Strong hands pull me backward and press me against the wall. "Stay there," the voice commands.

One of the hotel's security guards goes to Rob to help him to his feet. I'm assuming the guy holding me is one too. Cold metal wraps around my wrists. He pushes my new brackets tight, then turns me to face him.

"Mind telling me what this was about?" The man, a grandpa in his sixties, crosses his arms. The younger rental cop, a kid my age, pulls out his notepad.

I look past the man in blue to my woman. She's on her feet, a mask of armor in place, but it doesn't hide the swelling of her lip or the bruise forming under her left eye. "You okay, Starlight?"

Senior Cop looks over his shoulder, noticing Harper for the first time. His eyes widen and he hurries to her side."You all right, Miss?"

She holds up her hand to stop the man. Her gaze bounces from Rob to me, to the rental cops, and back. "Are you a cop?"

"No, ma'am. Hunter and I run security for the hotel," he says proudly.

Hunter, the younger dude, rolls his eyes. "Mind telling us what's going on?"

"I will if you uncuff him." Harper points to me.

Senior Cop shakes his head. "No can do, Miss. The hotel has a strict no fighting policy. I have to escort him off the property or call the police."

"But that's not fair! He was defending me."

"Is that so?" Hunter asks.

"Yes! Pull the security footage." She points to the cameras and both security guards look up.

"You know what," the older guy muses. "I think I will. Hold down the fort, Hunter. I'll be back in a jiffy."

I lean against the wall with zero intentions of causing anymore trouble. Guilt gnaws at my conscience. Ethan is going to kill me. I ruined his best man's face and just got myself kicked out of the wedding. That only leaves Cash, Gemma's brother-in-law, as a groomsman. Harper's probably out too, but her face wasn't my fault.

"So," the younger guard, Hunter, says, easing over to Rob. "You're a woman beater?"

Rob spits blood at Hunter's feet.

Hunter smirks, then socks Rob in the stomach. "Where I come from, we respect the ladies in our lives."

Rob bends over and rests his hands on his knees. He gasps for air, his eyes watering.

Hunter comes over to me and twirls his finger. I turn around. He uncuffs me and tucks his buddy's shackles into his back pocket. "Between you and me, that man deserved worse, but you can't stay. Rules are rules and while I support what you did, I'm not getting fired over it."

Harper runs to my side. I tuck her under my arm and nod to the man. "I understand."

"The lady can go up to your room and grab your things, but you gotta wait outside. Past the sidewalk or else Frank will call the cops on you for trespassing after being kicked out."

I hold Harper tighter. After what she's been through, I don't want to let her go but I don't have a choice. My clothes aren't important, but I need my keys and wallet. Everything else can be replaced.

"I'll get them," she says. "I'll get everything."

Harper kisses my cheek and heads toward the elevators. Rob stands and makes a move like he's going to follow her.

"I don't think so." Hunter pushes Rob back a step. "You're not going anywhere until that girl is back in my sights. That's how ladies get killed, and I ain't having her life on my conscience."

"You think I'm a murderer?" Rob laughs.

"You ain't got a problem beating a woman. What's to stop you from taking it too far when no one's looking? Nope." He shakes his head. "Sit your ass down before I take Frank's cuffs and slap them on you."

Chapter 14

HARPER

IT'S easy to hide the aftermath of a night with Rob.

Bruises can be covered with makeup and ice reduces swelling. These are the things I learned the first few months of being with that man. Just like I learned that his apologies were empty promises and although he swore it would never happen again, somehow it did.

At some point, I began to believe I deserved to be hit. If I was a better girlfriend, or a better lay, his boss would take more money off the debt. Or if I kept the house cleaner we could live somewhere that wasn't a dump. Rob wouldn't be so skinny if I learned what a proper meal was. Somehow, all of his problems became my fault and I believed it when he told me so.

Two years ago I was sent to rehab for a drug and alcohol addiction.

My accidental overdose almost took my life, and in the same breath it saved it.

Did I have a problem with drugs? Yes, but my addiction wasn't the root of my problems. The drugs and the drinking were the coping mechanisms I used to deal with my depression and anxiety. In the six months I was committed, I learned how to manage my feelings and cope when things got hard. I realized that while I was to blame for my decisions, the catalysts that brought me to that day weren't my fault.

Just like what happened today wasn't my fault.

I tell myself this even as my mind tries to justify Rob's actions. I wore a slutty dress. I bit him. I tried to hit him. Everything he did was reactory if I make him the victim. Those things are what I did, but I have to remember what I didn't do too.

I didn't ask Rob to kiss me.

I didn't invite him to touch me.

And even though my dress is short, that doesn't mean it's an invitation to assault me.

Rob is not the victim today, I am.

I knock on Ethan and Gemma's door. I feel terrible. Their wedding will be ruined. One groomsman looks like he survived a horror movie, the other is kicked out of the hotel. I'm sure I don't look too great either. With less than twelve hours until the wedding, they need to know what's happened.

Ethan's in his boxers when he opens the door. "What fucking time—" He stops mid-sentence and stares at me eyes wide. "Jesus, Harper. Are you okay?"

He opens the door wider and walks to the vanity inside. He grabs the ice bucket and dumps half its contents on the counter. He lifts the plastic baggy out and ties a knot, securing the cubes left in it, then hands me the makeshift ice pack.

"Thanks."

"What the hell happened?" He closes the door behind me.

I tell Ethan everything, starting with roping Noah into fake dating me yesterday all the way up to this morning. I leave out the details on the beach, but he understands where we went. When I'm done, Ethan runs a hand through his hair and sits on the edge of the bed. "Goddamn it, Harper."

My heart squeezes. Everything that's gone wrong this weekend is my fault. I'd like to say I wish I would have stayed home, but I'm not sorry. Being here brought Noah and I back together. It sucks that Gemma and Ethan's wedding suffered, but I wouldn't take anything back. Still, I feel guilty. "I'm sorry."

"No," Ethan says immediately. "Shit, I didn't mean it like that. None of what happened is your fault, and just so you know Noah told me about you two yesterday. I'm glad y'all finally got together, it just sucks." He takes a breath and sighs. "What are you going to do?"

"Me?" I ask surprised. "I'm not the one getting married today. What are *you* gonna go?"

He shrugs, a lovestruck grin on his face. "I'm going to marry the woman of my dreams. Does it suck my friends won't be by my side, sure, but that's life. It deals shit hands from time to time, but that doesn't mean we stop playing the game. What I want to know is, what are *you* going to do, Harper? Are you going back to Georgia or are you gonna stick around this time?"

"I don't know," I tell him truthfully. "Everything is so new. I thought Noah and I would have a few days before crossing that bridge."

"Want some advice?"

"Sure."

"I promise, Noah will be supportive no matter what you choose, but long distance is hard. Stay." Ethan holds his hands out to me. I toss the ice pack onto the vanity and let him hold me. We were friends at one point. Not the huggy type, but we had our moments over the years. "Noah will offer you the world and I need you not to overthink things. Just say yes. Give him a shot. A real one. I promise, you won't regret it."

I nod and Ethan pulls me into a hug. He kisses my forehead in a platonic way then sets me free. I leave him and go to Noah's hotel room. My bag is still packed from yesterday and his is mostly together. I grab the few things we had in the bathroom, check that I have both our car keys and his wallet, then head down stairs.

Rob is still being babysat by the security guard, only this time the older one is giving him a verbal lashing. I wave my hand to let the younger one know I'm done and he gives me a curt nod.

Noah waits for me on the street's edge, a step off the hotel's property. He reaches for our bags and holds them in one hand while looking at me. I haven't seen myself yet. I refused to look in the mirror when packing our things, but I'm sure I don't look great.

"I told you I'd break his nose before the weekend was over," Noah says lightly.

I laugh because if I don't, I'll cry. "You did, didn't you."

"Come here, Starlight." He drops our bags to his feet. I step into his arms. The weight of today is wearing on me. I want to take a shower and crawl under the blankets, but remember that I'm still homeless, the room refund hasn't hit my bank yet, and we've been kicked out of our hotel.

Noah rests his cheek on my head. Even when we were younger he was taller than me. I never caught up to him. Kinda glad. We wouldn't fit as well together if I had. "Ethan texted me," he says. "Told us not to worry about the wedding."

"I feel so bad."

"Don't." Noah carefully pushes me back and meets my gaze "I know what you're thinking, but none of this is your fault. Rob is a dick who got what he deserved and we got each other. All things considered, I'd say the weekend was a win."

"Mind sharing your rose-colored glasses?" I tease.

He shakes his head and grabs our bags again. We walk to the parking garage and find our cars. Mine's on the fifth floor because I self-parked to save money instead of valeting it.

Noah escorts me the whole way up, despite us passing his truck on the second floor. When I pop my trunk, he sets his suitcase alongside mine, overlooking the extra bags of clothes and the few personal belongings I have.

"What now?" I ask.

He leans against the side of my car and smirks. "You come back to my place and we plan for the rest of our lives."

"That sounds great, but seriously though. We need a plan."

"I am serious." Noah turns and drops down on one knee.

My heart hammers in my chest. I can't breathe, can't think. We've only been together for a day. People don't get married after one day! Then again most couples don't have the history we do. It could work. *It won't work.* But we could try.

Noah takes my hand and looks up at me. "Maybe I wasn't clear last night, Harper, but I love you. I never stopped loving you. Will you do me the honor and..."

He hesitates and I think I'm going to explode with anticipation.

I don't know what to say when he asks.

Yes?

No?

Maybe?

"Will you be my girlfriend?"

I let out a heavy breath and punch Noah in the shoulder. I don't know if I'm relieved or frustrated, but I'm something. "You're a dick."

He stands and pulls me into his arms. His lips caress my shoulder, kissing me tenderly. "You haven't answered yet, Starlight."

I thought it was obvious. I'm crazy about Noah. I guess I always have been, which is why I never let him go. In hindsight, it makes sense why Rob hated our friendship. Noah and I were endgame and Rob was the shitty half-time show. We were always meant to be together, which is why I take Ethan's advice and say yes.

Six Months Later

HARPER

The day after the wedding Gemma called me. She cried, apologizing profusely for what happened. We talked as Ethan drove them to Miami for their cruise. Really talked for the first time in forever. Turns out, she was holding just as much back as I was, but Rob was wrong. I was wanted at the wedding and every other event they had up to it. Gemma was afraid I'd say no which is why she never asked and thought if she talked about everything I missed out on that Rob's new girlfriend was a part of, I'd run away again.

She's not wrong. I probably would have canceled on her, so I'm glad things worked out the way they did.

Lydia dumped Rob within minutes of hearing what he'd done to me. Turns out, he was beating her too and she had the pictures to prove it. He didn't take the breakup well which landed him back in security's hot water, only this time she pressed charges. Something I never had the courage to do.

I moved into Noah's condo that weekend. It was supposed to be temporary, just until I found a job and a place of my own, but as the weeks went by I didn't want to go anywhere. Being with him feels like home and thankfully he agrees.

Until recently, I didn't know he rented out his house in Palm Beach and moved down to Fort Lauderdale while I was in rehab. Just like I didn't know he gave up a full-ride to Florida State after high school to stay local because I was coming back. Turns out, Noah did a lot of things for me that I didn't know about and finding out years later made me feel like shit, but I can't change the past.

If I could, I'd go back, shake the stupid out of my younger self and save myself an insurmountable amount of heartache.

What I can do, though, is shiver my ass off on the only cold day Florida will have this year while waiting for Noah. He was supposed to be here twenty minutes ago and even thought he said he's running late I'm waiting.

He pulls into the parking space the condo designates for him and jumps out of his truck. "I'm so sorry, Starlight. I left ten minutes later than I should have and got stuck in traffic."

Noah dips his head and greets me with a kiss. When he sees me shivering, he opens the backdoor of his truck and grabs a jacket from under the seat. He keeps at least two in there at all times because he knows how easily I freeze.

I stick my arms through the sleeves and link our fingers together. "Come on. I have a surprise for you."

Noah lets me lead him through the first floor of his building and to the beach. He stops when he sees the candles and the roses spread out to say *will you marry me*, just like they were in our fake engagement story. He looks at me confused. "What is this?"

"This is me calling you out on the big game you talked." I take a breath. Hot damn, this is hard. I'm so nervous I'm shivering and sweating all at once. I don't have a speech, although now that I think about it I probably should have planned one, maybe bought him a ring too. All I have to offer is me. "Marry me, Noah. You know you want to."

"No," he says without faltering.

I look up, not believing he shot me down. I didn't mean today. I meant in the future. It felt stupid to tell the world he is my boyfriend when he is so much more. He's my world. My rock. My best friend. The word fiancé or husband doesn't even feel like enough, but it's better than boyfriend.

And he said no.

Noah reaches into his pocket and pulls out a velvet box. "I was going to save this for Christmas, but now's as good as any."

He lifts the lid and inside sits the most beautiful diamond ring I've ever seen. "You're not stealing my moment. Marry *me*, Harper Dianne Herron. Marry me and give me lots of little children and make me the happiest man alive."

"You stole my proposal," I tease, unable to stop smiling. Noah shrugs. He doesn't wait for me to say yes. He takes my hand and slides the diamond over my finger. It sits on a white gold band, the only thing I've ever said I wanted because yellow gold makes me look sickly, and fits perfectly. "How long have you been carrying that ring around for?"

"Exactly twenty-eight minutes."

One Year Later

HARPER

Noah and I had a shotgun wedding at the courthouse two months later.

We didn't invite anyone.

I thought it would be better that way. Less chances for something catastrophic to happen, but we did have a reception at Gemma and Ethan's house that weekend. Rob wasn't invited, but Lydia was. We've stayed in touch and she's become a good friend now that our ex is out of the picture. She, Gemma, and I don't see each other often but we have a group chat and try to meet up once a month. Lately though, it's been harder than usual to make the drive.

I lie in bed, unable to find a comfortable position. Sheriese (Reese) Morgan Ruckers is too big to stay in my belly, but too stubborn to come out. The perfect mixture of Herron and Ruckers, just like her name. A token to each grandmother so she'll always be connected to family.

I tuck a pillow under my side, but it doesn't help the pressure on my back. Everyone I know said pregnancy was amazing. They're wrong. It's nothing but smelly farts, weird cravings, and the constant need to pee. But it'll be worth it because Noah and I can't wait to welcome Reese into our life.

Noah hands me a bowl of cookie dough ice cream with chocolate magic shell and gummy bears. He takes a bite, stating he needed to make sure it wasn't poisoned then sits next to me. I cuddle into his side and baby girl moves closer too. I swear, she's already a daddy's girl and she isn't even here yet.

I'm okay with it because I'm wrapped around him too.

I never believed in perfect, but Noah and I come close, and close is more than I ever thought I'd have.

More From Bailey

Broken Love Series

1. Beautifully Broken

1.5 Paper Hearts

2. I Hate You, I Love You Part 1

3. I Love You, I Hate You Part 2

Stand Alones:

Unexpected

Falling for You

In Too Deep

Fantasy Novels by Bailey Black

The Lost Darling

Second Star to the Right

Now Available

I've sworn off men forever!

Okay, not forever but for a few months. After my last hook up, my vag needs a reset because the last man to touch me broke it in the worst of ways. Not a problem, until my new dance partner comes into the picture. He's turning into my forbidden fruit, tempting me in ways I didn't know possible.

I have three months of celibacy ahead of me and eight weeks to whip my new dance partner into shape.

Someone save me.

Who knows. Maybe I can win Harlow over. Maybe she will finally see me.

Being in love with your best friend sucks

Find it on Amazon

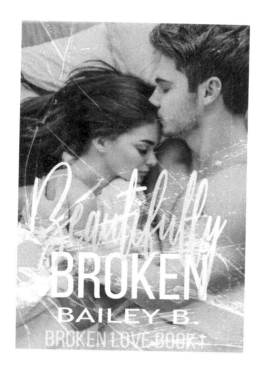

Now Available

Most people don't think about the day they'll die. They coast through life, blissfully unaware of how their time is ticking away. I wasn't like most people. I welcomed death, wanted her to take me away from the prison I called life, but she refused. I tried twice only to survive. And then, when I thought I had nothing left it came.

A reason to live.

Rex was a small, unexpected ray of light my world of darkness that blossomed into a beam of sunshine. I thought, maybe this was why Death didn't take me. Maybe she knew that if I held on a little longer things would turn around. But the third time Death came to my door wasn't by choice. Someone else brought her, and I fear this time she might take me.

Rex

Being the son of a country star sucks. My parents are never around, I move every year or so, and I have no real friends. Everyone around me has an agenda. Everyone except Piper Lovelace. I can't get that girl to notice me. Trust me I've tried.

Thankfully, fate stepped in and gave me the break I needed. I've got her attention, now I need her to give me a chance.

CHAPTER 1

PIPER

I'm the school slut. It's a title I wear, not proudly, but because it's what's expected of me. Everyone at St. A's High School knows my bio-mom's a whore—a real screw-you-for-money whore— that slept with the physics teacher last week.

Thank you, Facebook, for tagging me in that humiliating article.

Not.

Bio-mom was arrested for all of two seconds before making bail thanks to her pimp and the John she got caught with, he also happens to be my first period teacher this year. So, on top of the normal whispers spread about me on the daily, that mess is going around too.

It's fine.

I'm used to my name being in everyone's mouth. It's been that way since the third grade. Back then, people talked about my dirty nails, how skinny I was, and how my best friend was a boy. In high school, the daily gossip changed to where I moved to, what alleged drugs I was on, and eventually who I had spread my legs for. When the rumor started that I gave a killer blowjob for fifty bucks, no one doubted it. Why would they? I'm the girl with a whore for a mom. The girl from the wrong side of the tracks.

Literally.

There's the rich side of town where my classmates live, the good side, the tracks, and then *that* side. It's like the shadowy place in the *Lion King* Simba was warned to stay away from. Yeah...bio-mom lives there.

Anyway, not long after that rumor about me started, I figured what the hell. They say when life gives you lemons, make lemonade. I was given stupid, horny boys. So, I made money.

For the record, I've never actually touched anybody. At first, I turned everyone who approached me down. But there were a select few I eventually said yes to. The most selfish, conceited, disrespectful guys in our school got special treatment.

Underneath the shadows of the stadium bleachers, they dropped their pants. Exposed their less-than-exciting-junk to me. And then I kicked them straight in the balls. Those jerks fell to their knees, cursing my name while I took all the cash from their wallets. It was the perfect hustle.

Anyway, all of this is why I'm being stared down by Tad Parker. Captain of the baseball team, running back on the football team, and total tool. Bloodshot eyes narrow on my face, expecting a different answer to the question asked this morning.

"It's still a hard no, Tad." I stop walking and cross my arms.

While I'd love to take the pretty boy for all he's got, I'm trying to turn a new leaf and make the most of what's left of my senior year. I don't expect to fix my reputation, but I'm trying to change the way I see myself. Which means no more pretend illicit acts for money.

Tad rolls his bloodshot eyes and pulls a brown leather wallet, that probably costs as much as a year's tuition, from his back pocket. He thumbs through his cash, offering more twenties than I've held in my entire life. "Come on, Piper. I'll make it worth your while. Five hundred. Right now for five minutes in the bathroom."

Tad's a good looking guy, if you're into that classic blond-haired, blue-eyed, prince charming wannabe look with the attitude of Gaston. He has no shortage of self-entitled princesses throwing themselves at him.

I shake my head and push his arm back. My checking account may be teetering on the edge of zero, but I'm not this desperate. "Why not hit up one of the JV cheerleaders. They'd jump at the chance to get tangled up with you. For free."

"Because they aren't Piper fucking Lovelace. Now come on." Tad's hand curls around my arm. He squeezes, pulling me towards the stadium bathrooms.

One Mississippi.

My airway constricts. Bats swarm in my stomach, threatening to bring up the vending machine cinnamon roll I had after fourth period. I absolutely detest being touched; it sets off a catalyst of reactions that steadily get worse. My one and only thought at this point is to make Tad let go.

I dig my heels into the ground and yank my arm back, but my efforts are useless. I try to pry his fingers off me, punch him, kick him in the leg. Nothing I do makes a difference. Tad's too strong. Even with my best attempt at a struggle, he drags me clear across the parking lot almost effortlessly.

Two Mississippi.

My hands tremble, sending vibrations up my arms and throughout my body. I need help. I hate asking for help almost as much as I hate being touched, but I don't have much choice. I look to my left and then my right, but there's no one in sight. No one to hear my screams. I try anyway, opening my mouth to yell, but nothing comes out.

This can't be happening. I swallow the tiny bit of saliva in my bone dry throat and try again.

Nothing but air.

Beads of sweat drip down my neck as the feeling of impending doom lingers. The memory of a crooked grin I'll never forget flashes before my eyes, amping the intensity of my breakdown.

I spent a good part of this year in counseling to learn how to manage my panic attacks. Finding ways to keep everyone from noticing my freak outs. Tad makes me feel like I'm trapped, watching from the outside, as I lose all control.

Three Mississippi.

Logically I know it's been more than three seconds. It has to have been, but I'm stuck in a time warp. Everything happens at a snail slow pace yet lightning fast at the same time.

Tad pushes me against a wall near the entrance of the girl's bathroom, just outside of the football stadium. He lets go of my arm and presses his hands on either side of me. I realize that this situation probably isn't going to end well, but my anxiety begins to subside. As close as Tad is, he's not touching me anymore.

I can think again.

Feel again.

Pain surges through my arm like a lightning bolt. It was probably there the whole time, but I didn't notice. I'm going to have five little bruises from the pressure of his fingers but I don't move to soothe the throbbing. I hold my ground, fists balled at my sides, and stare up at him.

"I'm not above dragging you into the bathroom, but I don't want to do that. I just need you to go in there with me, Piper." Tad rests his forehead against the wall. His breath loud and shaky beside my ear. "A thousand dollars," he says suddenly, turning his head, begging me with his eyes to concede. "Walk in there with me. Please. You have to. "

If my heart wasn't already racing, it would be. That's a lot of money, enough for a ticket out of town and a few nights at a cheap motel. It's not nearly enough to pay my bio-mom's debts, but it would put a dent in it and maybe keep everyone off my back a little longer.

I don't know though. Whatever rumor is bound to start about me would be gone in eight short weeks, but this situation doesn't feel right. Something's off. "I need that money. More than you can imagine, but no."

Tad beats his fist on the wall beside me. I flinch, but he's so lost in himself he doesn't seem to notice. "What the fuck, Piper? I've offered you ten times more than your worth. If you don't go in there, I'm gonna be..." He shakes his head.

"I don't want—"

Tad turns to me again, this time crashing his lips onto mine. He tastes like cigarettes and tuna fish, two things I hate. His hands push into my hair, tangling and pulling my roots. Bile creeps up my throat.

I don't want this.

I don't want him.

No! I bite down on the tongue that's invaded my mouth and press my palms to Tad's chest, pushing as hard as I can. He stumbles back a step and stares at me, wide eyed, apparently shocked that I rejected him.

"You bitch!" He raises his hand and slapping me across the face. "You don't want to do this the easy way, fine. We can do it—!"

"Hey!" A deep voice booms from my right. A wide, tall body comes out of nowhere, physically shielding me with its massive frame while a hand shoves Tad's shoulder.

Tad loses his balance and stumbles a step to the right. "The fuck you want, Montgomery?"

Rex Montgomery—owner of said voice—reaches behind him and puts a protective hand on my hip. With everything that's happening, my brain doesn't seem to register the touch. It can't, it's too stunned that *he* of all people came to my rescue.

I mean, the man is a living work of art. At six-foot-four, Rex towers over damn near everyone at St. A's. Teachers included. It's a known fact that he played ice hockey at his last school, and rumor has it he's already been drafted to go semi-pro next season. Needless to say, every inch of him is carved from gold. Not really, but I hear his muscles are drool worthy. Add to that near perfect body a strong jawline and an angled nose. Yeah, girls swoon just from hearing his name. I'll admit, I might be one of them, sometimes, but never in public.

"Leave her alone," he growls.

Tad snorts. "That's cute. You sticking up for the trash. This bitch doesn't belong here, Rex. All girls like her are good for is a quick lay."

"Fuck you," I yell. Rex squeezes my hip, probably trying to be reassuring. Oddly enough, it works. A calm settles over me, releasing an unexpected smile.

What the heck is happening right now?

"Tell you what, you can take her into the boys bathroom first. When you're done I'll do my thing with her in the girl's. My treat, man."

Without warning Rex swings, catching Tad off guard with a right hook to the eye. Rex moves like a shark. Agile. Quick. And with precision. He swings again, hitting with enough force to knock Tad back a step.

I stand there like an idiot. Mouth open. Eyes gaping as if this is the first time I've witnessed two boys throw down. I've seen fights before. Hell, my tattoo artist runs a backyard fight club once a month that once upon a time I used to go to.

But this is different.

The rage in Rex's eyes is unlike anything I've ever seen. It's terrifying and unbelievably hot at the same time. I couldn't tear my gaze away even if I tried.

Tad grunts and lunges forward, hitting Rex in the stomach with his shoulder, but he barely moves. Rex punches him in the side, once, twice, then slams Tad's face onto his knee.

Tad falls to the ground, panting, blood seeping from his nose and a cut on his brow. He took a hell of a beating, and I have no clue how he's still conscious. Must be all that practice getting his ass handed to him on the football field. Defeated, he holds a hand up in surrender.

All of this is going on and I'm over here, less than three feet from the action, fighting the urge to jump up and down like a freaking cheerleader. Something has to be wrong with me today. I've never been the preppy ra-ra type. I'm more of a glare at you from a distance kind of girl. But watching Rex kick Tad's ass has me feeling some kind of way.

"Since you were too stupid to listen the first time, I'll tell you again. Piper's closed for business," Rex growls. "You will not stop her in the hallway or corner her when she's alone. Your days of talking to or thinking about Piper are done. If I find you in the same room as her outside of class, I'll kick your ass three ways from Sunday. Got it?"

All the bubbly feelings I had watching Rex kick Tad's ass disappear. Reality smacks me in the face with a horde of questions.

What does Rex mean by the first time?

Is he the reason everyone has left me alone the last few weeks?

What the hell is going on!?

Tad spits blood onto the ground and nods. "Got it."

"Good," Rex says rising to his feet. "Now get the hell out of here before I beat the living shit out of you again."

I watch Rex while he watches Tad walk away, guarding me until that low-life is out of sight.

Rex turns. His dark brown hair, short on the sides but long enough to run your fingers through on top, blows in the rare Florida breeze like a damn shampoo commercial. Under normal circumstances I'd make fun of him for it but I'm too stunned to speak. My mind's still tripping over the fact that *he* saved me. That he touched me and that my pulse is racing faster than a greyhound from the way he is still looking at me.

"Are you okay?" Rex takes my chin between his thumb and forefinger to examine my face. My breath catches. Not because I'm anxious, but because the feeling of impending doom isn't there. There's no tightness in my chest or nervous shakes. No needles shooting down my spine or fuzziness in my head. Instead, there's an electric current pulsating between us that I've never felt before, similar to my anxiety needles yet different.

"I'm fine." I'm not fine. My skin's on fire, the space between my legs aches, and I'm a confused mess. Rex is the first person to touch me this year who doesn't send my body into shock. His skin on mine should ignite a catalyst of crippling reactions. Instead, heat spreads from my cheeks down to my core. Awakening parts of me I thought died long ago.

Rex drops his hand. Deep blue's study me, combing over every feature, making my insecurities bubble up. The bags under my eyes. The scars on my arms, some hidden beneath a colorful tattoo, others still visible to all who look beyond the dozen rubber bracelets.

"Wanna get out of here?" He asks with zero traces of hidden innuendo.

Another first. The only time guys—who aren't the Harris twins—talk to me is to ask for a favor. An unfortunate hazard of my reputation.

Please don't let Rex ask a favor.

"Piper?"

Shit. I must have zoned out. No, I don't want to leave with you because I don't know what's going on with me! I shake my head, hoping I didn't actually say those words aloud.

Rex smiles revealing two deep, beautiful dimples.

The overwhelming need to have his hands on my body consumes me. Tears prick the back of my eyes again because for the first time in a year I want to be held. What's worse, I want to be comforted by him— the hot almost stranger who saved me.

I hate it.

I like it.

I don't know how to take it. I've gone so long learning how to cope with the anxiety of unwanted touch that I forgot how to react when it's desired. I look up at Rex, feeling like a complete idiot, unsure of what to do next. Should I say thank you? Is that enough? I mean, what he just did, saving me, is huge!

"Can I walk you inside? I'm sure Cooper wouldn't want you by yourself after that bullshit. And I..." he rubs at the back of his neck. "I don't want to leave you alone. You know, in case Tad comes back."

"Okay." My voice cracks, sounding nothing like its usual calm, collected self. Rex steps closer and tucks me under his arm. There's a bubble in my chest but I can still breathe. Still function.

I think I'm nervous.

Go figure. The hottest guy in school that I'll *never* have a chance with is ushering me inside and *now* my brain starts to act like a teenage girl. If I can't get this under control, I'm screwed.

Rex angles his body to shield me from eyes that might be watching as we cross the parking lot. The smell of musk and clean linen swirl in my head. It's delicious. I sniff again, committing the scent to memory because the likelihood that I'll be this close to him again is slim to none. Even if Rex can touch me without causing a debilitating panic attack, handsome, popular guys don't actually like girls like me. They just like the way we make them feel.

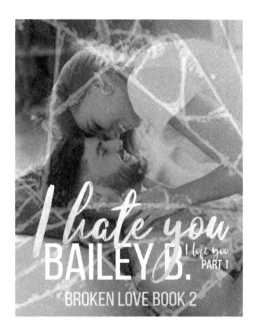

I Hate You, I Love You Part 1

Now Available

They say when you meet the person you're supposed to be with, time stops. Your brain takes in every micro-detail, committing it all to memory, and you're hit with this unexplainable need. A need to get to know that person, talk to that person, simply be beside that person. And then there's the kiss. A fire spreading, earth-shattering, kiss that wipes all others from your memory. I've felt that pull towards someone once, and it consumed me. But it wasn't for love, it was hate. I absolutely, without a doubt, HATE Logan Harris.

CHAPTER 1

LOGAN

I run a shaking hand through my hair, dark strands slithering like snakes against my palm. I thought my new neighbor looked familiar, but I couldn't figure out why. At first I didn't give the girl much thought and assumed the familiarity was because we had hooked up or something. But that round face and those long dark locks haunted me all night. And then, passing her on the way to first period this morning, the scent of rosewater shampoo set fire to my neurons.

My middle school best friend, Danika Winters, has returned home after more than three years and instead of being thrilled, my skeletons are knocking.

I swallow a lump in my throat the size of a cannon ball. My heart's racing. Vision's blurring. Suddenly, I'm a seven-year-old boy again, sitting in my therapist's office, his icy fingers curling over my shoulder. I shudder and blink back the first round of demons haunting me.

Feelings I've fought for years bubble in my chest. I can't risk Danika running her mouth and anyone finding out what happened. No one besides me, her dad, and the two other men in that room know the truth.

I intend to keep it that way.

Twisting an unlit cigarette between my fingers, my gaze drifts to Danika as she enters the cafeteria. Watching her amble to the food station with Sarah Archer, I don't know how I missed it. She looks exactly the same as she did in middle school, only older. Same olive skin. Same hazel eyes. Even the singular dimple on her left cheek when she laughs is still there.

I watch, with a sick sense of deja vu, as Danika bypasses lunch entirely, instead opting for just a Coke. Lunch was our thing back in middle school: sitting on the stage, sharing a peanut butter and banana sandwich, and a soda. I still remember the day she told me her mom was sick. She cried the whole lunch period, never once touching her half.

Being the nosy fuck that I am, I've noticed there's only one car in the driveway next door. Now knowing that Danika is my neighbor, I'm guessing her mom died. Whatever they were doing in California that kept them gone for so long apparently didn't work, and I doubt it was cheap.

Tad Parker sits on the tabletop beside me. "You look like you're out for blood. Who was stupid enough to piss you off this early in the year?"

I don't particularly like Tad but being on the same football team all throughout high school has forced us into a strange sort of friendship. He thinks we're friends, and I don't. I slip the cigarette I've been playing with between my lips and light it up. "No one."

Trays settle on the table behind me. I don't need to look to see who's sat down. Tad only hangs out with a specific group of entitled pricks and no one would dare to enter his circle without being invited.

I scan the cafeteria again, searching for Danika's unique hue of brown. It's a rich shade, filled with natural highlights. She's always had a color too pure to be from a bottle, something I didn't appreciate when I was thirteen.

I take a drag of my cigarette and exhale a cloud of smoke above me. I've got to stop thinking about Danika like this. Like she's still the girl I ate lunch with every day for three years. The one I told all of my secrets to. The girl who used to be my best friend.

Danika is my enemy because she may know what happened that night, and I have to remember as much. I take another drag and hold my breath, letting the smoke singe my lungs. Focusing on the burn in my chest makes tuning out the cafeteria chatter easier.

Until I hear her name.

"You guys remember Danika." Sarah sets her tray beside Tad and looks at my tablemates. "Right?"

There's a collective murmur of uninterested hellos, meaning no one remembers who Danika is. Good. She'll have to prove she belongs and judging by the fact she still wears Converse sneakers; Melody is going to eat her alive.

Melody Fox, self-crowned queen of St. Anastasia's High School has earned every bit of her title: bitch. I can't stand the bitch, but for some reason she seems to think we are a thing. Exclusivity isn't in her vocabulary, so I gave up fighting her on it last year. I still get to fuck who ever I please and she…I don't know what she gets out of the arrangement. I don't care either.

"You're like, really pretty," Melody taunts, setting a trap Danika is sure to fall into.

I almost feel bad, but Melody is making my job easier. Danika was always a quiet girl and cowered when met with confrontation. I highly doubt that's changed. I give it a day, two tops, of being on Melody's radar and then she'll find another lunch table to sit at. Hell, maybe she'll find a new school while she's at it.

"Who does your hair?"

"Um." Danika runs unmanicured fingers through her long strands. "I don't dye it."

"So that's natural?" Melody snickers.

Her best friend Rachel Moore cackles beside her. They glance at each other, a silent conversation in the works. I've never understood how girls do that, communicate with each other with nothing more than a look. Guys don't put in that much effort. If we have something to say, we say it.

"She's probably too fucking poor to dye it," I add on an exhale. The words feel heavy on my lips, but I can't stop thinking about what Danika might remember. I need her on edge, and possibly even a little afraid of me. Maybe then I can intimidate her into staying quiet. "Have you seen where she lives?"

"No! Where?" Melody gasps.

Another drag. Another exhale to numb my mind and the shiver of guilt rippling through me. "The fucking shack next to me."

"You mean Mr. Andrew's old guest house?" Melody titters.

The weight of Danika's stare burns my skin. I turn my head and glare at her because she needs to realize that I'm not the same timid kid she left behind.

Sorry Dani.

"Whatever. Poor or not." Gunner Wells cuts off Melody's infectious hyena laugh. He looks at Danika, gaze settling on her massive rack then finding her face again. "You're fucking hot."

Danika isn't hot, she's beautiful. Always has been. Only now, she's grown into her body. She developed early. I know that's strange to say but come on. I'm a guy. I notice these things. Especially on a pretty girl who leaves her table to sit with the weird friendless kid who had a stutter in the sixth grade.

That kid was me.

Awkward as fuck, thick rimmed glasses, and quieter than a church mouse because damn near everyone picked on me when I talked.

I was in therapy for years to correct my speech. Although, looking back, I'm not sure if those sessions helped my situation or made it worse.

Tad crushes his soda and tosses it at the trash can. It circles the rim then falls onto the cafeteria floor. He grunts, probably remembering how shitty he was on the basketball team as a freshman. "Yeah, at least she's not like Piper."

"Don't fucking talk about Piper," I quip. Tad smirks, realizing he's gotten under my skin and I'm reminded once again why I can't stand him.

Piper Lovelace, my on-again-off-again foster sister, doesn't deserve to be treated the way she is. Part of her reputation is my fault, I started the rumor that she was a slut as a joke last year, when I considered her to be nothing more than a nuisance. Before I knew what she was going through. Not that that's any excuse.

I never expected the rumor to stick because most of the things people say about Piper are forgotten in a day or two. It didn't help that soon after she started hanging around with a bunch of different guys adding fuel to the rumor fire. Even so, everything they say about her is wrong. Piper is a good person, she's just been dealt a shitty hand in life.

"Let me guess, Piper's fucking both you and Cooper now that she's moved back home again?" Tad digs a joint out of his cigarette pack and lights it, not giving two fucks about the cafeteria monitors. They won't do shit anyway, a perk of going to the most expensive school in the county. *Certain* kids could probably murder someone in cold blood on campus and damn near get away with it.

Tad sucks in a breath, holding the smoke in his lungs then passes the rolled paper to Gunner and says, "Tell me, is that bitch as good in bed as the rumors say she is?"

I toss what's left of my cigarette to the floor and jump off the table, ready to kick Tad's ass, but Cooper—my twin brother— beats me to it. He comes up from the left, catching Tad in his blindside and throws a jab at his face. Tad falls off the table and clutches his cheek like the little bitch that he is. Serves him right. Piper is family and you don't fuck with family.

I sit on top of the table again and light another cigarette to calm my nerves. I'm anxious, full of unused adrenaline and need something to take my mind off stomping Tad's face into the pavement.

"Fuck!" Tad yells, but anyone within earshot has gone back to talking with their table mates. Everyone on campus knows that if you fuck with Piper, talk to Piper, hell even look at Piper the wrong way, you'll face the wrath of Cooper. He's more protective of her than a starved watchdog with a steak.

Our principal, Mr. White, grabs Cooper by the arm and escorts him to the office with Tad in tow. Mom's going to be pissed when he gets suspended for the rest of the day but she'll understand. She always does. Cooper spends more time out of school than in and she barely bats an eye. But when I get in trouble, all hell breaks loose.

Melody groans and rolls her eyes. "Always with the drama."

From my peripheral vision, I see Gunner make himself comfortable next to Danika. I don't like the way he's looking at her, the way he's whispering into her ear. How she playfully shoves him and they both laugh. I have no right to be pissed, but just being around her sets me on edge.

Besides, I saw her first.

I Love you I hate you Part 2

Now Available

I fell in love with my next door neighbor when I was eighteen. It was fast and crazy and the best experience of my life, until I got pregnant. Logan, he pushed me away when I needed him most. Without his support, I made the hardest decision of my life and then I left. I ran away to start over with no plans of looking back. Only now I have to go back. My dad is about to marry his mom and it's just a matter of time until my secret comes out. When it does, everyone is going to hate me.

I Love You I hate you is the second book in the Duology. If you have not read Part 1, please do so first.

Asher Anderson is a dick.

We aren't friends, so when he seeks me out in the cafeteria on the worst day of my life, I'm suspicious. When he tells Liam Heiter that we'er dating, which couldn't be farther from the truth, I want to kill him.

Until I see Liam's reaction.

Liam—my best friend, the guy who crushed every hope of us *officially* being together —is jealous. He has never looked at me this way and I love it.

So, I play along.

Maybe watching me with someone else will make Liam suffer like I have the past four years. And maybe, just maybe, he'll come to his senses and realize we belong together.

It's not like I actually *like* Asher. At best, I tolerate him.

What's the worst that can happen?

Find It on Amazon

CHAPTER 1

Maggie Mills, my best friend since freshman year, hip bumps me then leans against the cold metal lockers that line B-hallway of Ridgewater High School. Her lips pull down into a frown, disapproving dark eyes narrowed into slits. "You're staring again."

I force a smile and close my locker door, forgetting the chemistry notes I opened it for. I leave the spiral bound paper inside, tucked between my English Lit book and my Pre-Calc folder. Grabbing them now will affirm Maggie's suspicion that I was indeed staring at Liam Heiter and press play on her broken record of disapprobation. "Was not."

Maggie turns her head to me, ruby red lips pressed into a thin line. She's quiet, watching me scrutinize the expression that's clear as day on her face. Whatever she's about to say, I'm not gonna like it. "Did you hear? Liam asked Corah to prom. Seems like things are getting serious between them."

I choke on air that lodges itself in my throat but twist the sound into a meager laugh. Liam Heiter—my other best friend, the one I've known since diaper days—doesn't do serious. After a month, two tops, he breaks things off because those girls can't offer him what I can. Family. History. Love without strings.

I twist the cap off of my water and take a sip to settle my nerves. Corah Raymond is no different than any other girl who has tried to settle Liam down. She's the flavor of the moment, whereas what Liam and I have goes beyond words. Our relationship has built every year we've been together, blossoming from a booming friendship into an all consuming fire.

"There's only one way to find out if the rumors are true." I toss my water bottle at Maggie and pull my phone out of my back pocket.

I talk a good game, pretending that watching Liam with every girl who bats her eyes in his direction doesn't bother me when, really, it does. Even knowing he and I are endgame, the few weeks his arms wrap around anyone else is nothing shy of hell. I live for the moments he's single, when we can be together.

"Lee." I beam at the nickname I've used since before I could form real words. The nickname no one else is allowed to utter. I hold my phone up, pretending to record our conversation for the school paper I don't actually write for. I take pictures that never get used, but the extracurricular looked good on my college applications. "Comment for the paper?"

Liam lifts one corner of his lips into a lopsided grin. My heart flutters as his emerald eyes lock onto my boring browns. High school has been his playground because, not only does his personality demand attention, his good looks attract it.

While Liam grew into a walking god of a man the past few years, I, unfortunately, stayed the same lanky beanpole I've been since middle school.

My boobs came in and filled a smaller than average bra in the seventh grade but they forgot they were supposed to keep growing; my butt has just enough cushion not to hurt the chair; and my shoulder-length hair hasn't figured out that when I spend forty-five minutes straightening, blow-drying, and sticking every product known to man in it, it's supposed to stay pretty. I blame the Florida heat for that last one.

Most days I look like a pubescent boy who stuck his finger in a light socket. At least, that's what the popular girls tell me. The same popular girls who are currently glaring, wordlessly reminding me that I am not worthy of breathing the same air as them.

"Only for you," he declares. *Always for me.*

"Elaine," Corah purrs with a chastising smile.

I hate her. I hate her perfect hair and toned body. I hate how Liam's muscles flex beneath the sleeve of his shirt when he pulls her close. Most of all, I hate that she's at his side while I'm three feet away trying to remind her, and me, that I am important.

"Football season is over. What could the paper possibly need to know about my Lee Lee?" Corah pinches Liam's chin between her fingers and pulls his lips to hers. The kiss, while quick, is strategic. A show of power on her part. I may be reminding Corah that l was here first, but she's not going to let me forget that, for the time being, he's all hers.

My stomach twists inside itself. I usually avoid Liam when he's got a girlfriend, keeping our interactions to lunch and the confines of my bedroom. Watching him with someone else is too painful. And yet, here I am. *Keep it together, Lainey.* "Rumor has it, you two are going to prom together. Tell me how that happened."

Liam pulls back from Corah's embrace and narrows his ember eyes on me. He knows this conversation won't make it into the paper. This is for me. Sure, I could have texted to ask my burning questions, but I want to hear the truth straight from the horse's mouth. Most importantly, I want to hear that Maggie is wrong.

"I asked. She said yes."

"Don't be modest, Lee Lee." Corah giggles. She leans into him and presses her perfectly manicured fingers against his chest. Corah may be dense, but she is not stupid. She intentionally digs her knife deeper into my wounds, pouring salt with each detail I've yet to hear. "If the people want to know, let's tell them."

Corah pauses, waiting for Liam to spill the beans. When he doesn't, she is more than happy to do it for him. "It was last Saturday. Lee Lee picked me up for our night on the town like he always does, but I immediately knew something was off. He was too quiet in the car and he would barely hold my hand. When he pulled into Riverside, my gut twisted because everyone knows that is his breakup spot."

I stare at Liam, my eyebrows nearly kissing my hairline. Riverside Park is our special place and has been ever since we were kids. Every relationship he's been in has ended there because he was thinking about me.

Coming back to me.

I wait for some silent explanation as to why Liam would bring *her* there, of all places, but he breaks eye contact with me to stare at the floor.

"And when Lee Lee took me to the playground, I thought for sure we were done," Corah continues. "I followed him out of the car, practically tripping over my feet because my eyes were blurry with tears. And you know what he said to me?"

"What?" Please tell me, because I can't fathom why he would taint what's ours with this trash.

Corah looks up at Liam, doe-eyed, and smiles. "He said it was on the playground that he first fell in love."

Her voice fades into the background. My pulse thunders through my body with loud, almost deafening thrums. It takes every ounce of willpower I have not to run and jump into his arms but I can't do that because no one knows about Liam and me. We chose to keep our unorthodox relationship a secret so high school doesn't ruin it. Things between us aren't ideal and, to keep appearances, Liam has to date. I could see other people too, but it's easier if I don't.

I chew on the inside of my cheek and silently plead to the universe for Liam to look at me. He needs to understand that I love him too. I don't care if it took three years of secretly pining after him and another five years of him sneaking through my window late at night for us to get here, but his gaze is glued to the ground.

"That's why Liam took me there, because that silly playground was where he found his first love, and he thinks I might be his last." Corah clasps her hands over her heart, feigning happy tears.

Dark spots cloud my vision but, at the moment, they are better than tears because my internal compass is spinning in circles and I'm a ball of emotions. I want to scream. I want to yank Corah by the hair out of Liam's arms and then, of course, I want to cry.

Somehow I manage to force it all down—the humiliation, the self-pity, the tears, and most of all, the anger— and make myself smile again.

"I know what you're thinking," Corah beams.

No. I highly doubt she does. If she did, she wouldn't be hanging on the arm of the man I love. Gloating. She would be running, because the things I want to do to her, to both of them, aren't legal in fifty states.

"It wasn't a big, fancy promposal, but I didn't need anything glamorous. The way Lee Lee asked, it came from the heart and that's what matters most." Corah snuggles into Liam's side and looks up at him like the sun rises and sets because he exists.

I know it does in my world. I shiver, feeling a chill as the actual sun dips behind a cloud. Ironic considering we're inside and its rays barely shine through a nearby window. Still, I feel the darkness nonetheless.

"You must have been thrilled." I force the words out, dying a little with each syllable.

Liam finally lifts his emerald gaze to meet mine. There's no remorse in his expression. No regret for breaking my heart into unmendable pieces. What I find is worse.

Pity.

The bell rings and, for once, I couldn't be more grateful there are only two and a half minutes between classes. If I have to stand here any longer pretending to be happy for these two, I might crack.

"We should go," Liam says, leading both him and Corah towards A-hall. The same hallway I should be going to, but I can't seem to make my feet move. I can't bring myself to walk behind them and watch their happiness. Their circle of friends follow like peasants, eager for the attention of the king and his new queen. A few steps down the hallway, Liam looks over his shoulder at me. "See you tonight."

"Are you okay?" Maggie asks once Liam has turned down the hallway. Her hand reaches out and I watch her fingers touch my arm. I feel nothing. My mind is too busy keeping my head above the swell of tears and holding onto a smile to process anything else.

"Yeah." I don't sound like myself. My voice is strained, cracking with emotion while coming out an octave higher than normal. "I just need a minute."

Maggie's perfectly plucked eyebrows knit together. Everything she wants to say is written on her face.

Don't let that jerk get to you. He never deserved your heart. You'll get through this. Everything will be okay.

But she keeps it all to herself. "Alright. I have my extra credit thing with Mr. Alverson today, but I'll try to be done in time for lunch." She pauses, studying me a little longer. "Are you sure you're okay?"

I nod, my lips stretched tight across my face. The smile couldn't be faker, but Maggie doesn't press the issue.

After what feels like an eternity, she sighs and says, "Okay, sweetie. I'll see you later, but text me if you need me."

"Will do."

The moment she rounds the corner of B-hall, the dam of tears I was holding together with scotch tape and band-aids cracks. The world around me blurs into starbursts of light as liquid pain trails down my cheeks.

I run into the nearest bathroom and press my back against the wall. I squeeze my eyes shut, forcing myself to take slow, steady breaths—a tactic my therapist taught me back in middle school when my social phobia controlled my life. *Deep breath in. And let it out. One. Two. Three. Four. Five.* It takes a few cycles for the pressure in my chest to decrease and the waterworks to dry up, but eventually I start to feel better.

A toilet flushes in a nearby stall and the nervous needles under my skin spring back to life. I can't bring myself to look at who is here and see either a smug smile or a look of pity from someone who thinks they know what has happened. I keep my eyes closed, using eight-year-old logic of, *if I can't see you, you can't see me*. I know that's not how the world works, but it makes me feel better.

The lock on the stall door slides open, metal scraping inside itself. Heavy footfalls take one step, and then two, and then stop. Silence eats away at my resolve to stay strong and keep my eyes closed. After the slowest five seconds of my life, I hear, "You look like shit."

You've got to be kidding me!

My eyes snap open at the deep rumble that is uniquely Asher Anderson's. He's got this smoked-a pack-a-day rasp, paired with knee-knocking baritone pitch. If Snow White and the Prince ever had a son, it would be him. With hair as dark as a starless sky and moon kissed skin, the contrast is striking. But then you add in his eyes, a unique shade of amethyst that looks too perfect to be real. The girls around here all but melt at the sight of him. Liam may be the shining king of the school, but Asher is the prince wearing a crown of thorns.

Asher crosses the bathroom to wash his hands in the sink, shaking loose water droplets into the porcelain bowl when he's done, never breaking eye contact. Not even when he reaches for a paper towel from the dispenser.

"Get out!" I scream, unable to take his patronizing stare any longer. This is the girl's bathroom for Christ's sake. Is this man so heartless as to beat me here just to inflict more pain on my already bleeding heart?

Wouldn't put it past him.

I've known Asher all my life. Our parents—mine, Liam's, and Asher's mom—used to be friends. I still remember the stories my mother would tell about how excited she was for all of them to be pregnant around the same time. We were a heartbeat away from being a B-rated version of the sitcom *Friends* if they'd all had kids.

Until one day when everything imploded.

As for Asher and I, we drifted apart in the sixth grade after he ridiculed me for getting my first period. As if I wasn't embarrassed enough to find a puddle of red when I stood to jump into the pool, Asher let everyone at that birthday party know what happened. He even went as far as calling me shark bait the rest of the year. Liam thought it was hilarious. I wanted to die.

"Perhaps I should say the same to you." Asher chuckles and leans his ass against the sink, crossing his long, muscular arms.

My jaw drops. This is my bathroom. He… My train of thought is lost as I take in my surroundings. The girl's bathroom has more than two stalls and it doesn't have urinals.

No. No. No! I cover my face with my hands, mortified. *Could today get any worse?*

"It's cool," Asher guffaws. "No one will walk in on us if that's what you're worried about. Besides, it looks like you need a moment."

I let my hands fall to my sides, shoulders rolling forward. I know Asher's sympathy will come with a price, but I do need a minute's peace. I don't know how I'm going to make it through lunch and my next three classes. Everyone is talking about prom and now all I'll be able to think about is Liam and his stupid promposal. "It's girl shit. I'm fine."

"You don't look fine." Asher steps closer, crossing the tiny bathroom in only three strides.

I turn my head and stare at a phone number someone scribed onto one of the stalls. I hate looking at Asher. He makes my stomach jump and my heart flutter at the same time. One a feeling of irritation. The other… not going there.

Asher tucks his knuckle under my chin and lifts, forcing my gaze back to him. "You look like Liam stomped all over your heart. Again."

I jerk my chin free of his grasp and lean back against the wall. I'd rather touch the cream-colored tiles with all its grimy germs than him. I hate him. I don't hate him. I don't know how I feel about Asher. Things between us are… complicated. Always have been.

"You don't know what you're talking about."

"Don't I though?" Asher chuckles again. The dude laughs a lot, only it never sounds happy. There's always a hidden layer of darkness or sorrow or something straight up evil in it.

Asher steps back and grabs the door's handle. He tugs it open and steps out, leaving me alone in the boy's bathroom. I take a second to gather my thoughts, grateful to finally be alone.

I shake my head, irritated that he thinks he knows me. Knows what I'm feeling. Asher doesn't know jack shit about having a broken heart. He's the heartbreaker, just like Liam, leaving a trail of tears wherever he goes.

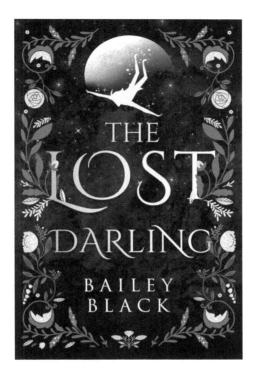

Second star to the left and continue until morning.

I got that line tattooed on my wrist the day I turned twenty-one. So much symbolism in such a simple sentence. At the time, it was a nod to the future and the infinite possibilities to come, while reminding me to remember the past and to look for magic in the world.

Growing up, nothing was ever what it seemed. The shift of leaves on a tree was a faery skipping by. Shooting stars were a chance to make wishes. Shadows were souls stuck between this world and the next, mirroring a life they once had.

My imagination was limitless, the world a wonderful adventure waiting to unfold.

It's easy to lose that sense of wonder with the weight of life on your shoulders and I wanted a reminder to get me through the hard days.

Most importantly, it was an ode to the boy who earned the title of my first crush, even if he was animated. Peter Pan wasn't a *save the damsel* kind of prince. He was daring, and selfless, and took care of the ones he loved. He was a friend to all but never afraid to fight the Pirates when their moral compass broke. Wendy was an idiot for leaving him. She rushed home to a heartless world full of men willing to lie through their teeth to get down her pants.

But that's the beauty of a book, the characters are perfectly flawed. Damaged just enough that we still love them. Whereas reality is nothing but empty promises and baggage the size of mountains.

The day I got my tattoo I would have given anything to be whisked away into a fairytale. My world was crumbling and all I wanted was to go back to when life was simpler. I didn't realize I had sealed my fate in ink.

Branded myself as one of the Lost.

Neverland was everything the stories made it out to be. Beautiful. Full of magic. Filled with handsome men and debonair pirates. But the author of my favorite tale left out one crucial detail.

In order to get there, you have to die.

Now Available

Thank You

To me, this is the hardest part of the book to write because there are so many wonderful people who help make each story come alive and every time I get to this page, my mind goes blank. So, don't mind me as I copy and paste from the last book.

First and foremost, I want to thank my BFF Alexandria James, who put her debut novel on the back burner to beta read/edit/help me not loose my sanity through out this process. Without her picking my brain and helping me to organize my thoughts, this book would still be sitting in my massive pile of incomplete projects. (Shameless plug…her amazing vampire paranormal romance is available in May!)

A special thank you to Elizabeth Murphy for being my star beta reader. I would be lost without your attention to detail and your suggestions.

My editor Beth at Magnolia Author Services… you ladies rock. Your attention to detail has this book polished and shining.

A huge thank you to my Mom for reading everything I write, even if it makes me cringe when she gets to the dirty bits.

To my kick-ass PA, Becky… you make it possible for me to focus on writing. Without you I'd be a squirrel of half thoughts, open giveaways, and with a dead Facebook group.

To my husband who likes to give me grief when I spend too much time typing but gets on my case when I haven't touched my computer for a week…I love you.

To the bloggers and bookstagrammers who bring my stories to the world. You are amazing! I cannot begin to express how grateful to you I am.

To everyone I'm sure to have forgotten because I'm Dory's second cousin twice removed and feel like I'd forget my head if it wasn't attached.

Finally, I'd like to thank my readers. Every time you open one of my books, you make my dream come true.

Thank you.

Xoxo

Bailey B.

ABOUT THE AUTHOR

Bailey B is an up and coming New Adult author. She lives in Lehigh Acres Florida with her husband, twin girls, and two fur babies. She enjoys (but doesn't get to take part in because of her crazy daughters) the simple things like Disney+ binge watching, Netflix romcoms, reading and sleeping. She reads two to three books a week and thinks if narwhal's are real animals then unicorns might be too.

Lightning Source UK Ltd.
Milton Keynes UK
UKHW020046110123
415109UK00016B/1109